HE LOVES ME, HE LOVES ME NOT

A hilarious, sexy and heartwarming romantic comedy...you do not want to miss this fun, feel-good romance.

— MARY DUBÉ, CONTEMPORARILY EVER AFTER

...refreshing, funny, emotionally charged, and very entertaining to read.

— CAROL, TIL THE LAST PAGE

There is humor, there is heart and there is heat in this story! I absolutely loved it! . . . Mari and Liam delivered. Yowza, their chemistry was palpable.

— BIBLIOPHILE CHLOE

PETAL PLUCKER

Funny, charming, and utterly captivating! I devoured this sparkling read.

— ANNIKA MARTIN, NEW YORK TIMES BESTSELLING AUTHOR

Petal Plucker was funny, entertaining, fresh and fan-yourself-worthy . . . Their enemies-to-lovers romance is both charming, tender and steamy, and you'll love both of these characters (and their families!) and their sigh-worthy happily ever after.

— MARY DUBÉ, CONTEMPORARILY EVER AFTER

Morland has created a masterpiece of a romance . . . one of my favorite [books] of the year.

— CRISTIINA READS

Humorous, raunchy, and refreshing, Petal Plucker has rightfully earned its way, in my opinion, as one of the best romantic comedy [books] this year.

— CAROL, TIL THE LAST PAGE

MY ONE AND ONLY

This book was gripping, well written & the chemistry between the characters sizzled throughout this wonderful read.

All I Want Is You

Another heartfelt, steamy, terrific story. This is an author who really knows how to create a story that catches a reader's attention and characters that capture her heart.

Taking a Chance on Love

Thea and Anthony are in for a surprise when it comes to the language of the heart . . . I am in awe.

Then Came You

This story really pulled all my heartstrings. This was truly a beautiful story and makes you believe there really is true love out there.

ALSO BY IRIS MORLAND

ROMANTIC COMEDIES

Oopsie Daisy

He Loves Me, He Loves Me Not

Petal Plucker

War of the roses

LOVE EVERLASTING

including

THE YOUNGERS

Then Came You

Taking a Chance on Love

All I Want Is You

My One and Only

THE THORNTONS

The Nearness of You

The Very Thought of You

If I Can't Have You

DREAM A LITTLE DREAM OF ME

SOMEONE TO WATCH OVER ME

TILL THERE WAS YOU

I'LL BE HOME FOR CHRISTMAS

HERON'S LANDING

SEDUCE ME SWEETLY

TEMPT ME TENDERLY

DESIRE ME DEARLY

ADORE ME ARDENTLY

OOPSIE DAISY

A STEAMY ROMANTIC COMEDY

IRIS MORLAND

BLUE VIOLET PRESS LLC

For Matt, who is unlikely to ever know I dedicated a book to him.

OOPSIE DAISY

CHAPTER ONE

KATE

Once upon a time, there was a girl who thought she could bang her brother-in-law's cousin and not have it come back to haunt her.

Oh wait, that was me. Katherine Lydia Wright, third sister of the Wright girls, the most brilliant, extraordinary, outstanding, and amazing of the three of us. My oldest sister, Mari, might be good at eyeliner and my other sister, Dani, might be good at buying potting soil on sale, but I was something else. You know those people who make you go: wow, she's going to accomplish so many things?

Well, no one's really said that about me except for my parents. They also told me I could grow up to be a honey badger when I was five. But *I* believed I was going to accomplish things. And isn't that what really matters?

Anyway, here I was, pursuing my dream of becoming a genetic engineer, starting grad school at the University of Washington, when it all blew up in my face.

Basically if you think of what happens when you light a

match near gasoline, that'd be an accurate representation of my life at the moment.

Here's a scene: me, a few weeks before my grad program officially started. I was meeting with my advisor that afternoon about my classes and my research goals. My particular type of research centered around modifying genes to create a biofuel that was like gasoline—wait, do you care about this?

You want to know about the cousin thing.

Patience, my friend. I'm getting there.

So here I am, about to knock on the door of my advisor's office. When I saw that he didn't have a nameplate, I realized I hadn't taken the time to look him up at all. Stupid me. I needed to do that when I got home.

I heard a muffled voice say *come in,* and I did. I saw a man with jet-black hair sitting at his computer, his face hidden by the wide screen.

Something in my stomach bounced. I called it my inner "uh-oh" voice, the same voice that liked to tell me that I should maybe not have put frogs in my sisters' beds because I ended up with frogs in *my* bed afterward.

"Have a seat," my advisor said. "I'll be with you in a minute."

I sat down. I placed my bag on my lap, but it tumbled from my grip when my advisor finally revealed his face.

Oh.

My.

Fucking.

God.

Lochlann. It was Lochlann. The man I'd had a one-night stand with three months ago. In *Ireland.*

Oh God, oh God, oh God. I'd had torrid sex with my advisor. I'd lost my *virginity* to my advisor.

Seeing his sharp features, his jet-black hair, that sensual mouth—it all came back to me in a rush. I'd never, ever forget that night.

But based on the way he was looking at me, he'd forgotten me already.

"Ms. Wright? You dropped your bag," he said coolly.

I looked at my bag, its contents having scattered near my feet. "Huh," was my brilliant reply.

"Are you all right?" he said a little more gently.

I bent down and began to toss my things into my bag— my phone with its eggplant emoji case, my feather pens because they were ridiculous, my keychains with one of my favorite science pickup lines. *I wish I was adenine, then I could get paired with U.*

He didn't remember me. *He didn't remember me.* I felt— relieved? Offended? Had I been that boring of a lay? God, how humiliating. Here I'd been, dreaming of him all summer, and he probably hadn't remembered my name the next morning. Even though we'd both been in my sister Mari and his cousin Liam's wedding.

Talk about awkward.

I stuffed my hands under my butt to hide their shaking. This only made my legs shake and I almost shook myself off the chair.

"Um, I'm Kate," I finally said, sticking out my hand. "You can call me that, too. No one calls me Miss Wright. Besides, I prefer Ms. anyway. I'm not married, although why should it matter? It's dumb. Men are just mister, no matter what."

I clapped my mouth shut, a hot blush staining my cheeks. Lochlann took my hand in his firm grip, and fuck me if I didn't have a mini-orgasm right then.

"Dr. Gallagher, nice to meet you." He sat back in his chair and sifted through the small handful of papers currently sitting on his desk. "I apologize for the mess. I was only recently given this office, but the previous occupant took all of the file cabinets and folders."

He put on a pair of reading glasses, which only seemed to emphasize his handsomeness. I also had to bite back an awkward giggle, because who called four pieces of a paper a "mess"?

But no, who cared about papers. More importantly, how had I not known that Liam's cousin was a professor in my field? Or that he was living and working in Seattle now? When I'd asked Mari about Lochlann back in June, she'd said he worked in Dublin doing something "nerdy."

Thanks a lot, Mari, I thought wryly.

"Oh, yes, I remember now. You're researching biofuels, which would make perfect sense as that is also my area of research."

My ears perked despite the situation. *Talk nerdy to me, Lochlann,* I thought with a shiver. And in that Irish accent? Swoon. He was going to have to mop me up after this, because I was already melting into a swooning-girl puddle.

"Your schedule looks good, although I'd encourage you to take more outside your specific field," said Lochlann—no, Dr. Gallagher, I had to think of him as that from now on. He was my advisor.

"I didn't want to overload my schedule with too many different types of classes, I guess."

Dr. Gallagher took off his reading glasses, and I almost sighed. "I'd like you to expand beyond your specific interests. It'd also look good if you plan to apply for an internship over the summer."

"I'll consider it."

"Excellent." He leaned back in his office chair, cool as an Irish cucumber. Or an Irish potato—except he was hot, so he was a very *hot* potato—

"Miss Wright, did you hear me?"

Me being me, I blurted, "Nope. Not one word."

Most people would've smiled, or rolled their eyes and huff-laughed. I tend to get people to do that, even when they find me annoying. It's a gift.

Apparently Dr. Gallagher was immune to me. Except in the sex department, or the memory department.

"Please pay attention," he said. "I don't have time to repeat myself."

"You seem *very* busy." I glanced at the four pieces of paper on his desk with a raised eyebrow. Okay, maybe I'd miscounted: there looked to be all of five documents. Damn, this guy sure was slammed with work.

Again, he didn't react. Was he made of stone? What had happened to the charmer who'd charmed my panties right off of me three months ago? Maybe Dr. Gallagher was impersonating his secret twin brother and the man sitting before me was, in fact, someone else.

Except when I looked at his wrist, I saw that scar, about two inches long, that I'd asked him about. *Get in a fight with a rosebush?* I'd joked.

Worse, he'd said wryly. *A very angry and overheated container of fuel.*

Right then, he saw me looking at the scar and moved his hands so I could no longer see it.

His gaze then flicked over me, and if I weren't imagining things I almost could've thought he *did* recognize me. It wasn't like we'd fucked without ever turning on the lights. I'd gotten a good look at him—head, chest, dick, legs. Ass, or arse, as he called it. And he'd done the same for me (except for looking at my dick, obviously).

But that gaze flicker of his disappeared so quickly I wondered if I'd imagined it. Was I hoping for something that wasn't there?

Does it matter? He's your advisor. Like this can go anywhere. Don't be totally stupid, Kate. Or even stupider than you've already been.

To be slightly fair, I didn't know he'd end up being my *advisor*.

The combination of being miffed and irritated with his arrogance made the reckless side of me come out to play. Which meant that the uh-oh voice rang alarm bells in my head. It jumped up and down. It said, *Kate, don't do it. Don't do the thing.*

"I most definitely don't have time for cheeky grad students," he said, steepling his fingers.

"Didn't you see that bit on my CV? 'Cheeky girl, can be bribed with snacks.'" Sitting up straighter, I added, "Speaking of running out of time—I'm meeting someone, so I can't stay much longer. My boyfriend, actually. He doesn't like when I keep him waiting."

Lochlann turned back to his computer. I hadn't imagined that heated look he'd given me. He recognized me, the dick.

Kate, he can't exactly bring it up. Come on.

He doesn't have to act like he doesn't know me, I countered.

"If you have any more questions, please email me," said Lochlann.

I was dismissed.

You know that feeling you get when you're so pissed your brain goes dark and words are suddenly just coming out of your mouth?

"My boyfriend, his name is Steve. He's a grad student, too. He's really smart. Like, he could win a Nobel Prize smart."

"Fascinating," said Lochlann. "Is he in the materials program as well?"

"No, he studies—" I struggled to think of a suitably cool and amazing thing to study that would make Lochlann jealous. Out of the corner of my eye, I saw the keychain I'd bought at the zoo a year ago: a wind-up flamingo that flapped its wings. "The mating habits of native Washington flamingos."

At that, Lochlann finally looked at me. "Flamingos? I wasn't aware they were native to the Pacific Northwest."

"Oh, there's a huge population in Forks," I said, naming the town made famous by the *Twilight* franchise. "They're everywhere. A real nuisance. They're basically like geese except they're pink. Super aggressive. Never approach a flamingo from behind."

"Fascinating," drawled Lochlann.

"But Steve—my boyfriend—he also plays football. He's *so* good at it. He works out every day and he can hit the ball *so* far. It's amazing." I knew I was digging my hole deeper, but my mouth just kept moving despite the uh-oh voice screaming in my mind to stop.

"Really? What position does he play?"

Shit. I didn't know anything about football because it had always seemed boring and stupid to me.

"You probably wouldn't know, since I'm talking about American football," I said breezily.

"I'm aware, Miss Wright. What position?"

Sweat dripped down my spine. I couldn't think of one position besides the one that came tumbling out: "The ball toucher."

"The ball toucher," repeated Lochlann, skepticism lacing his voice.

"Touching balls—it's very important."

Was that a bit of a smile on his lips, or was Lochlann just twitchy? "I can't say that I disagree with that statement."

Okay, I needed to get the hell out of here. Grabbing my things, I said hurriedly, "I'll call you. No, email. I don't have your phone number. Why would I have your phone number?" I laughed, but it came out as a croak.

"Have a lovely rest of your day, Miss Wright. Be sure not to get into any fights with a flamingo."

Oh my God, I'm so fucked.

CHAPTER TWO

LOCHLANN

Christ, I was fucked.

The second Miss Wright shut my office door behind her, I slumped into my office chair and groaned.

What were the odds that one of my grad students would be the same woman I'd slept with three months ago?

A woman who I later discovered was my cousin's new sister-in-law, not just one of the bride's friends. Luckily, Liam hadn't found out. And I wasn't about to tell him. He'd rip off my bollocks and throw them into the Pacific Ocean.

So I'd done what any self-respecting man trying to preserve his bollocks would do: I'd acted like I hadn't recognized her.

That night in June, when I'd found Kate drinking alone in an Irish pub, I'd been like a moth attracted to a flame. She'd been so vibrant, so unconcerned with what other people thought of her. She'd mimicked my accent, and it had been such a bad impersonation that I'd almost choked from laughter.

I hadn't laughed like that in a long time.

But I'd known then it had just been for sex. Hot, quick, dirty sex. No regrets there—Kate had given as good as she'd got. And when she'd gone back to the States a day after the wedding, that had been that.

Apparently not. She was like a bad penny I couldn't shake. Also a penny that blathered when it got nervous. Had she been like that back in Ireland? Because this Kate wasn't the confident woman I'd been instantly attracted to. She'd seemed so…young.

And that made me feel like such a damn creep. I reminded myself that she was old enough to be admitted to a graduate program. It wasn't as if I'd had sex with a high school student.

Let's stop that train of thought before we get arrested. God knows Americans love to throw people in jail.

I sighed. Should I ask Kate to be assigned to another professor? But what reason would I give?

We fucked each other's brains out a few months ago. It won't happen again. But it's a little awkward now. You get what I mean?

"Knock, knock," said a voice before my door was opened. Dr. Elizabeth Martin, one of my new colleagues in the department, stepped inside, her brown pumps clicking against the floor. "We're all going for drinks. Did you want to join us? We're going to a place that has some great Irish food."

Doubtful, I thought, missing the greasy pub food from back home fiercely. "I have more work to do," I said. Seeing Dr. Martin's disappointed expression, I added, "Sorry."

Americans were so bloody sensitive. Tell one *no*, you were busy, and they were liable to burst into tears.

"Come on, take a break. The quarter hasn't even started

yet." Dr. Martin sat down on the edge of my desk, crossing her tanned legs, her skirt short enough to reveal a bit of thigh. "You don't want to overwork yourself already."

I could hear the flirtatious note in her voice. Were all American women out to torment me?

Stop complaining, ye gobshite.

I could hear the voice of my dad in my mind, and I had to bite back a smile. He'd always been the traditionally Irish father: cursing you, even when he was offering praise. I'd had to learn through trial and error that most people didn't enjoy being insulted when you were trying to give them encouragement or advice.

Dr. Martin's skirt seemed to inch up her thigh of its own volition. Sneaky, that skirt.

Of course, it made me think of a different skirt on a different dress, in a different country and with a different woman. I could almost hear Kate's moans as I kissed down her spine, licking at the small of her back and kissing the faint constellation of freckles there.

I had to shift because my trousers were getting tight.

"See, you're already working," said Dr. Martin. She crossed her ankles and somehow managed to push her breasts together. The buttons on her blouse would burst off her shirt like shrapnel if she weren't careful. "You definitely need a break."

"I need to get this done."

She frowned but was undeterred. "I was surprised the department assigned you the one female student. I was so sure they would've given her to me."

You and me both, I thought darkly. "Our research coincides more than yours does," I said frankly, because it was true.

11

Although she was researching genetic engineering, I'd learned at the recent staff meeting that her focus was on agriculture.

"Just don't get yourself in trouble," she said suddenly.

I looked up sharply, but Dr. Martin just laughed.

"I'm kidding. You seem totally aboveboard, Professor." She snagged a Post-it from my desk and scribbled on it. "Here's my number if you change your mind about drinks. See you later."

I tried to clear up my inbox, but I could barely concentrate. Anxiety churned in my gut. There was no way Dr. Martin had seen anything between me and Kate. Fear wasn't the most logical emotion, however.

Grabbing my things, I almost dove under my desk when I heard Dr. Martin laughing down the hallway. Christ, she'd drag me along to drinks if I weren't careful.

So much for getting to know your coworkers, idiot.

Fucking sue me. I didn't feel like talking to people tonight. I needed some time to think and to figure out how the hell I was going to deal with a little problem called Kate Wright.

When I arrived home at the tiny flat I'd found a mile from campus so I had an excuse not to learn how to drive (Americans were bloody insane drivers), Clurichaun greeted me at the door.

A huge, fluffy orange beast of a cat, Clurichaun had been surprisingly calm about the whole move from Ireland. He hadn't remotely lived up to his name, an Irish fairy that loved to drink and play pranks. When I'd had to take Clurichaun out of his carrier at the airport, he'd blinked sleepily and had promptly fallen back asleep in my arms.

My flat consisted of a futon that was about to fall apart any day now and a coffee table made from a cardboard box. The living room was also my bedroom. *I should probably get some furniture…* I thought for the hundredth time. But it wasn't like research professors were paid decent money here. The only reason I'd swallowed the paycheck was because the University of Washington had one of the best materials and science programs and it'd be worth it to further my own research.

I'd known that I'd wanted to become a scientist since I'd discovered in primary school how easily you could create chemical reactions from basic things. I'd used up all of my mam's vinegar and baking soda one summer when I was five years old, loving the way it bubbled in her huge cooking pot like a cauldron full of potions. My mam hadn't taken kindly to me using up all of her ingredients, or using her cooking pot for science experiments.

As I'd got older, I'd become more interested in genetics and the science behind essentially engineering DNA. Combined with a real fear of climate change and the necessity to find a fuel source that wasn't based on fossil fuels that damaged the ozone, I became obsessed with the possibility of creating a type of fuel through genetic engineering. It was the combination of biology and engineering that I found fulfilling.

My work at the University of Ireland had brought great advancements in my research: specifically in experiments on bacterial DNA. As my research had progressed, my star had risen as well, and when I had the opportunity to go to a university with a larger, more robust, program, I hadn't hesitated.

But all of that hard work, the sacrifices, the paperwork and bullshite you had to deal with to immigrate to America —it was all in jeopardy. Because of one slip of a girl who'd shown up in the last place I would've ever expected her.

What were the odds? I laughed, because it was preferable to bursting into ugly man tears. I hadn't cried since my dog had got hit by a car when I was seven.

Clurichaun got onto my lap and started purring so loudly he made my knees shake. I stroked the cat's fur absentmindedly.

I couldn't let Kate know I recognized her. Most importantly, I needed to talk to Dr. Martin and see if she'd take her and give me one of her students. I didn't know the protocol in the department for a student swap, but I'd come up with some excuse. I'd say that Kate and I didn't get along. Or that she wanted to work with a female professor. That was plausible, right?

And how are you going to get Kate to agree to this?

Based on how embarrassed she'd looked during our bizarre conversation, I couldn't imagine she wanted to keep me as her advisor, similar research or no. My anxiety calmed somewhat.

I'd get this all hammered out and no one would need to know. As long as Kate kept her mouth shut—who would believe her, anyway?—I could keep my job and not have my reputation utterly fucked. I wasn't going to let one mistake ruin everything. One night of casual sex was not going to destroy everything I'd worked towards.

Clurichaun meowed in annoyance, hopping down to the floor. Apparently I'd been petting him too aggressively. He licked at his fur, his eyes flashing disdain.

"Sorry, mate. What would you do in my situation?"

Clurichaun just started licking his nonexistent bollocks in reply.

My phone rang, reminding me that I had a phone call with my mam and da tonight. It was about six hours later in Ireland at the moment. I made myself smooth my expression. I couldn't let my parents be suspicious. My mam, when she sensed something was up, would be like a hound on the scent for blood.

"Lochlann!" said my mam. Both she and my da's faces came up.

Da waved and then asked, "Can you hear us?" He practically yelled the words.

"Yeah, I can hear you. Da, you don't need to yell into the phone, you know," I said.

"Last time we called we couldn't hear you. Reception is terrible here," said my mam.

In their sixties now, my parents had worked their entire lives to give me the education they'd never had. As an only child, I'd got their complete focus, but with that came the expectation that I'd make something of myself. I wanted to become successful so I could support my parents as they aged. It was my duty as the only son.

"How was your day? Are you teaching yet?" said my da.

"Classes haven't started yet," I replied. "I told you that."

"Oh, well, I can't remember all the details of your schedule. Do you like Seattle? What's everyone like? Are there really Starbucks on every corner?" This from my mam.

I bit back a smile. "Seattle is kind of like Ireland, except

15

there aren't as many pubs. But the weather is similar. And yes, there are Starbucks on every corner."

My mam elbowed my da, my da wincing. "I told you! Have you been to—what is it called?—Walls-mart? Is that what it's called?"

"Walmart. And no, there isn't one in Seattle proper," I said with a smile.

My mam gave me a disappointed look. "Well, you need to go to one and tell us all about it. I've heard they're huge."

"Mattie, he's busy. He doesn't have time to go to a bunch of stores," said my da.

I told my parents about my new department, the classes I was teaching, and I briefly touched on the grad students I'd be advising. When I mentioned one was a female, my mam jumped on that detail, to my immense frustration. Although to be fair, the percentage of women in most STEM programs was abysmally low.

"A girl! Did you ever advise a girl in Ireland? I thought only men attended these programs," said my mam.

"It's not like they're not open to women," I countered.

My da pushed up his glasses. "No, but it's a field that men do. Like women are nurses."

I wasn't about to argue that things had changed and that there were plenty of men becoming nurses and women becoming engineers. Instead, I just said, "Well, there are women in the program. I met with my student today. Her research is similar to mine, which is why she was assigned to me."

"Is she single?" My mam's eyes widened. "How old is she?"

I needed to end this conversation now. Giving them an

excuse that I was meeting up with a colleague, I ended the phone call and sighed deeply.

Clurichaun meowed at my feet.

"What a fucking disaster," I muttered, Clurichaun seeming to nod in agreement.

When I was younger, I wished my two older sisters were two older brothers. Brothers didn't stick their noses in your business, or act like they knew *so much* by virtue of the fact that they were a few years older.

Okay, I was seven years younger than Dani, and nine years younger than Mari. Growing up, I'd seen them both as adversaries and the two people I wanted to impress. Which was why I put frogs in their beds or dyed their hair blue (makes sense, right?).

"Are you excited to start grad school?" said Mari serenely, her milky white hands resting on her burgeoning baby belly as we waited for our brunch entrees to arrive.

Mari was glowing, and it was almost to the point of being nauseating. Dani sat next to her, checking her phone, dirt under her fingernails. Mari had recently begun working as a freelance makeup artist and YouTuber, while Dani ran my family's flower shop, Buds and Blossoms, with her fiancé, Jacob.

My stomach roiled. Apparently Mari was literally nauseating, because I definitely felt like my stomach was about to come out of my butt.

The nausea was probably from thinking about the fact that I'd slept with my advisor and I had no idea what the hell I was going to do about it.

Yeah, I wasn't telling my sisters that tidbit.

Dani shot me a strange look. "Are you okay?"

"Totally."

"So, are you excited?" pressed Mari in that older sister voice. *You can't ignore me* was its underlying tone.

I almost felt badly for her husband, Liam. But Liam made me think of Lochlann, and oh God, I couldn't puke here. Had I gotten the flu somehow? In September? Maybe it was cholera or dysentery. I'd blame Lochlann for either of those diagnoses.

I shrugged at Mari's question. "Sure."

Dani was still looking at me strangely. "You're acting weird today."

"Am I?"

"You're so…" Dani tilted her head to the side, her curly hair gently waving in the breeze. "Calm."

"I can be calm," I shot back.

"The only time you're calm is when you're asleep, or when you were high on pain meds after getting your wisdom teeth out." Mari chuckled. "You thought Oprah was going to bring you an elephant as a reward, remember?"

"You cried so hard when Mom told you Oprah wasn't coming," said Dani.

"I did not," I grumbled, crossing my arms.

"But did you sign up for your classes? What are you

taking? Not that I'd understand any of it." Mari put up her hands, smiling wryly. "You're smarter than all of us."

At that, I sat up a little straighter and began to rattle off my classes. When my sisters' eyes started to glaze over, I sat back and smirked. They might be older but there were some things I knew about that they'd never get, like my fascination with genes and all the nerdy things that made me so excited but had bored them both to tears.

"Jacob says hi," said Dani as she texted one last message. "We're doing a wedding tomorrow and the bride has been calling us both nonstop to make sure we won't forget. Apparently at her first wedding, the florist showed up drunk and with a bunch of brown roses for her bouquet. She's been a little intense about this second round."

"Is that why she got a divorce?" I asked innocently.

Mari gave me the Older Sister Look. Dani, though, laughed.

"Worse," said Dani. "Her husband left her to live in a hippy commune in Hawaii. Apparently he renamed himself Rainbow Sunshine Cloudmaker. Suffice to say, Meredith didn't feel like joining him at the commune."

Right then, our food arrived. I always ordered waffles and mimosas for brunch, but when I inhaled the scent of delicious, golden, crispy waffle, my stupid stomach turned upside down. Couldn't a girl enjoy some waffles without it going badly?

Maybe I was just really, really hungry. I hadn't eaten since last night, and it was close to eleven AM. I drank a big gulp of my grapefruit mimosa, the bubbles making me cover my mouth to hide a loud belch.

"Lovely," said Mari as she began to eat her salad. "Always the lady."

"I try," I said.

I began to dig into my waffle, and for a moment my nausea disappeared. Mari began to talk about her baby shower in two weeks, which Dani and Mari's sister-in-law, Niamh (pronounced Neev, because sure, why not?), were planning. Dani had asked me if I'd wanted to help, but I'd declined. What the hell did I know about babies or baby showers? I'd bring the booze. That was the most important thing, anyway.

"I really don't want any games," said Mari. "Just gifts and food."

"Baby shower games are pretty stupid," agreed Dani.

Sounds boring, I thought to myself as I shoveled waffle into my mouth.

"Liam and I haven't agreed on a theme for the nursery yet. He wants to do something Irish, which I like, but I don't want a bunch of creepy leprechauns in my baby's nursery." Mari shuddered.

"Does Liam want to scar your kid for life?" said Dani with a laugh.

I added, "Maybe he's just really into Lucky Charms."

"No, he likes the original Irish fairytales but they aren't kid-friendly. He says he heard them growing up and look how he turned out. But since I'm pregnant, he always ends up doing what I say." Mari patted her belly with a wide smile.

Was it weird that all this pregnancy talk made me uncomfortable? I drank more of my mimosa, hoping my sisters couldn't see how bored I was. Which then made me feel guilty, because I loved my sisters and this was an exciting new chapter for Mari and Liam.

Maybe I just didn't get it. I didn't get the appeal of giving up your life, your dreams, your identity, for a baby.

I didn't know if it was the last bite of waffle or the second mimosa but the nausea returned full-force as we waited for the check. I started sweating profusely, and as I was about to run to the bathroom, that terrible heaving feeling took over.

I reached a nearby flowerpot filled with pansies and mums right before I puked up my waffle, my mimosas, and probably a kidney in the process. Nearby patrons gasped; I heard chairs squealing against the floor. Then I felt a gentle hand pulling my hair back as I vomited a second, then a third time. By the time I was done, I was sweaty, swearing, and mad that I'd just wasted a perfectly good waffle.

"Are you okay? Sit down." Dani directed me to a chair; Mari handed me a glass of water. I drank the entire thing in practically one gulp.

Mari put a hand to my forehead. "You don't seem like you have a fever."

"It's probably cholera," I joked.

"You'd have a fever then, you dork." Dani handed me another glass of water.

It took a lot of persuasion on my part to convince my sisters that the nausea had passed, and I could go home without them clucking and fussing over me.

I wondered if I'd gotten food poisoning—but didn't it take longer than that? I did feel better, though. Maybe it had been the waffle? Or I'd drunk my mimosas too fast?

"How was brunch?" asked my roommate, Naoko, as I

collapsed into a chair next to her. Naoko Tsushima was a senior, about to earn a degree in music. Her specialty? The tuba. Considering she was all of five feet tall, I still didn't know how she could manage an instrument that large. A flute would've made more sense.

"I puked my guts up," I said.

Naoko paused *The Great British Baking Show* episode she was watching. "Wait? Literally or figuratively?"

"Literally. Well, literally-ish. My actual guts are still inside me."

Naoko made a face. "Um, TMI. Also: why? Or what was it from?"

I sighed. "No idea. I'm guessing food poisoning."

"While you were eating? Or from food you ate last night?"

I shrugged. "I mean, what else could it be? I feel fine now. I don't have a fever. I can't imagine it's the flu, right?"

Naoko scrunched her nose up. "If you have the flu, I'm dousing you in Lysol." Pressing play on her show, she added with a chuckle, "You're probably pregnant."

I didn't even register her comment until I saw a commercial for baby wipes ten minutes later. I wondered if Mari was going to get fancy organic wipes for my niece or nephew. She was going to use cloth diapers, which sounded like a huge pain to me.

Then, a thought: *could I be pregnant?*

I pushed that thought down so hard, so fast, that I refused to examine it again. Except, it followed me the rest of the afternoon and into the evening.

Lying on my bed after the sun had set and listening to a super cheery podcast about how humanity was destroying the planet at an alarming rate, I couldn't get rid of the idea.

There was no way, though. Lochlann had used a condom. I'd seen him put it on and take it off afterward, so it wasn't like he'd tried to stealth me. Plus, my periods had always been irregular, so I could go six weeks before it appeared. When had I last gotten it, though?

I couldn't remember.

By the time I was peeing on a pregnancy test, sitting in a one-room stall at the one drugstore open at this hour, I could only see Lochlann's dumb, handsome face in my head.

I had to wait two minutes. I washed my hands three times just for something to do. I checked my phone, only to see Mari posting something on Facebook about doulas or midwives or whatever new pregnancy thing she was researching.

I ended up staring at the graffiti on the wall. One message read, *Steve is gay*. The next: *we're all a little gay, it's okay*. The third was just a drawing of a very long penis with a smiley face at the tip.

When I saw the *pregnant* message, I tossed the stick away like it was on fire. And because my life was just so awesome, it landed with a nice plinking noise in the toilet bowl.

"Are you done yet?" a man's voice called through the door. "Are you dead?"

"I have diarrhea!" I yelled. "You don't want to use this one!"

"It's the only one in the store, lady!"

I was already trying to figure out how I could fish out the pregnancy test without touching gross toilet bowl water. But

I didn't exactly carry a scoop or tongs for this particular issue. I could leave the test, but the thought of the guy on the other side of the door seeing it made me want to die inside.

Stress tends to make us fucking idiots—me especially.

I reached inside the bowl, fishing out the test, only to realize I'd been so distracted and intent on getting the test out that I'd forgotten to roll up my sweatshirt. It was now dripping wet and I couldn't take it off because I had nothing on underneath it.

"I need to piss, lady!" the asshole yelled as he banged on the door.

After grabbing the test and stuffing it into my back pocket, I wrenched open the door, my sweatshirt dripping water onto the floor. The asshole and I stared at each other for a long moment in silence.

"I clogged the toilet," I said finally, as if I needed to explain my red, sweaty face, my wet sweatshirt, or the water on the floor.

"Whatever, lady." But he tiptoed around me and then locked the door behind him so quickly that I let out a startled laugh.

I went home and peed on the second test in the box. Then the third. I lined up all three positive pregnancy tests on the bathroom counter and pressed my forehead against the cool mirror.

I was pregnant with my professor's baby, and he didn't even remember having sex with me.

CHAPTER FOUR

LOCHLANN

When my mobile went off for the third time in five minutes, I growled and almost tossed the stupid thing into the rubbish bin. Normally I put my mobile on silent when I was working in the lab, but I'd been too wrapped up in my work that I'd forgotten.

You'd think after my engagement had ended two years ago because I'd been too obsessed with my work that I would've learned my lesson. The day Sophie had tossed my ring into my face, she'd said, with little emotion in her expression, *You'll never love me as much as you love your work. I don't think you can love any woman. I'm not going to compete with your work anymore.*

I hadn't learned my lesson, though. I'd thrown myself into my work to the point that I hadn't so much as looked at a woman for two years—until Liam's wedding when I'd met Kate.

But Kate had nothing to do with love. It had been pure lust, an itch that had suddenly needed scratching. I'd always prided myself on my self-control. I'd never let myself be led around by my cock. I was rational; logical. I approached everything—from my work to my love life—like a scientist. Rationality in all things.

But apparently that particular approach had left the one woman I thought I'd loved cold.

Sophie and I had met when we'd been undergraduates in college. She'd been vivacious, beautiful, with a smile that was practically blinding. It hadn't taken me long to fall under her spell. Soon, we moved in together, and when I'd started my PhD program right out of undergrad, Sophie had been there for it all. The studying, the research, the hours upon hours of work I'd put into my dissertation. She'd been the first one I'd called when I'd got the news that I'd passed my exam.

Sophie had been patient. She hadn't pushed for us to get engaged. She'd known I'd needed to focus on finishing my PhD before I could consider settling down with a wife and eventually have children. Since she hadn't pushed, I'd assumed she was happy.

My mam had always said the smartest people never had any common sense, always in reference to me. While I was mixing chemicals to see how they'd react when I was a kid, I'd also forget to wear a helmet when I rode a bike or I'd stick my tongue to frozen poles in the winter simply out of scientific curiosity.

With Sophie, I'd fucked up; I'd taken her for granted. But it taught me that the likelihood of me finding a woman who'd tolerate being second place to my research was pretty much nil. Not because women were too demanding, or that Sophie had been asking for too much.

I just knew I could never give enough to any woman.

I was wrenched back into the present when I got a text message alert. *Come have drinks with me and Mari*, the first text from Liam read.

The second: *We're meeting at 7 at Patty's*

The third: just a bunch of beer emojis and the hands-pressed-together emoji.

My cousin was such a pain in the arse.

I didn't want to get drinks with him. Why? Fine, it had nothing to do with Liam: it had everything to do with who his wife was. I didn't need a reminder that I'd slept with her younger sister, and that younger sister was now my student.

I'd yet to speak with Dr. Martin about her becoming Kate's advisor. I'd been so busy with department meetings, orientations, and university paperwork related to my work visa that it had honestly slipped from my mind.

Or you're just ignoring the problem until it goes away.

Fine, maybe I was.

I was happy that Liam and I had reconnected, don't get me wrong. We'd been playmates as kids but after his da had left the family—my mam's brother—we'd lost contact with Liam and his sister, Niamh. I didn't have any other cousins besides them, and I was an only child. It wouldn't hurt to lean on family as much as I could.

Another message came through from Liam: *I know where you live.*

I snorted, and before I could second-guess myself, I replied that I'd come for drinks when I finished up my work in the lab.

When I arrived at Patty's a little after seven PM, it was already filled with college students. The quarter was starting in a week, and I'd watched as parents helped their kids move into the dorms across the street from my flat. Empty IKEA boxes cluttered the curbs, while music played well into the night as students partied the last week of summer away.

"Lochlann!" Liam practically shouted. A few students looked in his direction.

Loud, tall, and charming, Liam was almost my polar opposite, except for our similar Irish accents. His had softened and sounded more American to me since he'd lived here for over a decade. I'd teased him about it when we first saw each other in Ireland for his wedding. *You sound like a bloody Yank.* Liam had given me such a pissed-off look that I'd laughed.

"Liam, you don't have to yell. Hi, Lochlann. It's nice to see you again." Mari, her belly softly rounded now, stood and gave me a hug. She smelled like jasmine. Even pregnant, she was perfectly put together. I had a feeling that even with a newborn to take care of, she'd look amazing. My cousin was a lucky man.

Despite my best intentions, I couldn't help but see similarities to Kate in Mari's face. The sisters didn't look much alike, really, but they had similar smiles. Where Mari was tall and red-haired, Kate was small and slender with dark brown hair. It was Kate's eyes that drew you in: dark brown with thick lashes. She'd batted them at me back in Ireland and I'd been a goner.

"Have you been outside at all or do you live in the lab now?" said Liam, looking me up and down. "You look like a damn ghost."

"Liam, leave him alone. Besides, nobody gets a tan in Seattle," said Mari logically.

"You don't have to look like death, either."

I ordered a beer from the passing waitress. I'd probably need more than one tonight.

"What department do you work in again?" Mari sipped her lemonade as she looked at me. "I know it's something in engineering."

"Genetic engineering. Specifically in regards to biofuels."

Her eyes widened. "Wait, you must be in the same program as my sister Kate. You remember Kate at my wedding, right?"

Fuck me fuck me fuck me

Did I lie and say I didn't know if Kate was in my program? Or did I cop to her being my student? Sweat beaded on my forehead. Liam's eyes narrowed at me, but he wasn't a damn mind reader. He couldn't know the thoughts bouncing around inside my head.

"I'm her advisor, actually," I finally said quietly. "She didn't tell you?"

"I don't think so. But at brunch this weekend she was—" Mari bit her lip. "Well, she's been busy. As I'm sure you've been."

"She's a bright student," I said. *In so many ways.*

"Sounds like a conflict of interest," said Liam.

I gritted my teeth. "Why? We're not related."

"You're cousins."

"Cousins-in-law—so, hardly related."

"I doubt Lochlann would agree to be Kate's advisor if he thought there'd be an issue," said Mari. When the waitress returned with my beer and some onion rings, the food provided enough distraction to let the subject be dropped.

Mari started eating the onion rings, moaning and licking her fingers. Liam raised an eyebrow at her.

"Babe, save it for home," he joked.

Mari blushed to the roots of her red hair, but then pursed her lips. "I told you I was craving onion rings. I'm not going to apologize."

"Oh, you shouldn't. But I'd rather not have Lochlann here and everyone else watching."

I looked away from the two lovebirds, cooing like thirteen-year-olds on their first date ever. I was happy for Liam, don't get me wrong. Mari seemed like an amazing woman. When Liam had told me how they'd initially married, I hadn't been able to believe their relationship hadn't imploded. Drunken marriage in Las Vegas? That should've led to a quickie divorce.

Instead, Liam and Mari had married for real a second time and had a baby on the way.

When Sophie had walked out on me, I'd let the dream of a marriage and family go. The whole white-picket-fence thing wasn't for me. I'd accepted that a long time ago.

But that didn't stop a nip of jealousy to bruise my heart seeing my cousin and his wife together.

"Oh, Lochlann, are you coming to the baby shower?" said Liam suddenly.

I stared at him in surprise. "Why would I?" Weren't those things for women only?

"It's for all of our family and friends—men and women. Liam should be celebrating with me, too," explained Mari, delicately wiping her fingers on a paper napkin.

"I did help with the conception." Liam grinned.

I couldn't go. Not because of it being a baby shower—

and Christ, what would I even do there?—but because Kate would be there. She was Mari's sister: of course she'd attend. She was probably helping to plan it.

"I'll think about it," I finally said. "I might be too busy with work, though." *Mostly true, except I tried to take weekends off when I could.*

"If it makes you feel better, we're not doing the silly games people do at showers. I told my sisters not to plan anything like that," said Mari.

"What games would you even play? Pin the tail on the baby?" Liam guffawed.

"Worse: melt chocolate bars in diapers and guess what kinds they are."

"Wait, why—" I sat back in my chair. "Oh. That's disgusting."

"This is also why Kate isn't helping plan it. She'd have the absolute worst games just to be a pain." Mari sighed deeply. "I don't know if you know this, but my youngest sister is a bit…"

"Evil?" supplied Liam.

"Naughty," was Mari's reply.

I could confirm that Kate was naughty, but not in the sense Liam and Mari were talking about. My trousers tightened as memories flooded my brain. Sweat beaded on my forehead, and I took a long drink of my beer in the hope that it'd cool my horniness. But all I could see was Kate taking my cock in her small hand, stroking me from root to tip, her tongue swirling around the crown—

"Kate's always been a prankster," said Mari, breaking through my erotic memories. "I hope she doesn't do anything to make your life harder, Lochlann."

I choked back a laugh. God, if she only knew.

After I'd said goodbye to Mari and Liam, I walked home. It was about a mile-long walk, but the night was cool. I realized as a group of students passed by me that I needed to confront this situation head-on. Giving Kate to Dr. Martin would only create suspicion within the department, especially given the suddenness of it.

If I were being honest, I didn't *want* to hand over the student whose research was probably the most innovative of the entire first-year class. I wanted to tap into Kate's brilliant brain myself. I wanted to see how her research could complement mine, and vice versa.

Most of all, I needed to clear the air with her. Acting like I didn't recognize her would only lead to more drama. If I treated Kate as an equal, maybe we could avoid screwing up both of our careers.

I drafted the email to Kate within five minutes of arriving home. With Clurichaun purring next to me, I wrote and rewrote the email, asking Kate to meet with me, seeming to rewrite it a million times over until I finally sent the damned thing.

Now all I could do was wait.

CHAPTER FIVE

KATE

It took all of three days before Naoko sensed something was up with me.

"You're drinking tea," she said accusingly early on a Wednesday morning. "You hate tea."

I sipped my caffeine-free Earl Grey tea and cried inwardly. Taking a sip and trying not to cringe, I replied, "I don't hate tea."

"I distinctly remember us getting boba tea that one time and you almost burst into tears." Naoko sat down next to me and crossed her legs, giving me her *I'm onto you* look that she was so good at. "Then you threw the tapioca balls at me after we'd left."

My cup of tea had already turned lukewarm, and I set it down on a nearby table with a sigh. I'd been avoiding coffee because, according to Doctor Internet, caffeine would turn this fetus into a tentacled monster. Even though I wasn't particularly attached to the fetus, I didn't want to screw it over so early.

"I'm trying to cut back on caffeine," I said.

"There's caffeine in tea, you know."

I glowered at my roommate. "You know what? You can leave. I don't need your annoying facts right now."

Naoko pushed her glasses up her nose, the tip wrinkling. "What is wrong with you? You've been acting so weird lately."

"Have not."

Naoko held up her fingers and began counting them off. "One: you aren't drinking coffee. Two: you haven't wanted to go out and drink, which is usually your favorite activity. Three: I definitely caught you crying at a diaper commercial yesterday."

"It was a formula commercial."

I rubbed my temples. Since finding out I was pregnant, I'd done what any mature adult would do: completely deny that anything was happening. If I ignored it, then maybe it'd go away. Except for the whole avoiding caffeine thing. In all honesty, the smell of coffee made me queasy these days, and I was afraid my usual caffeine consumption could screw up this parasite inside me.

"Kate," said Naoko, bringing me back into the present. "Are you okay?"

Her voice was gentler, her expression so concerned, that the tears that I'd barely been holding at bay appeared. I started crying like a crazy woman, and Naoko, bless her, let me cry and just patted my shoulder. I think she even shushed me like a little kid.

"I'm. Pregnant," I wailed somewhere in between sobs.

Naoko's hand on my shoulder stilled for just a second before resuming. "Oh no," she murmured. "Who's the—" Her voice trailed off. I'd told her about my wild hookup in

35

Ireland, and she knew me well enough to know that I hadn't gone out with any other guy since then. I hadn't told her that my hookup was also my brother-in-law's cousin.

Because I needed to tell someone, and I was too afraid of what my sisters would say, I told Naoko the whole story: Lochlann being Liam's cousin; our hookup; and Lochlann being Professor Gallagher and my advisor.

Naoko's dark eyes widened to saucers behind her glasses as I spoke. When I'd finished, the tears had stopped. I sniffed and wiped my nose, feeling a little better.

"Shit," was her only reply after my confession.

"Pretty much."

"You're knocked up by your professor. That's almost impressive. Only you, Kate. You should get a medal."

"I didn't know he'd end up being my advisor at the time!"

"Yeah, but you get into these scrapes like no one else I've ever known." Naoko sat back and crossed her arms. "Are you going to tell him?"

"Don't I have to?"

"No—I mean, if you aren't keeping it. If you are, then that's another conversation."

I laid my head against the armrest. "I don't know what I'm going to do," I said honestly. "I'm still coming to grips that this is happening."

I'd assumed I had to tell Lochlann I was pregnant, but Naoko was right: it was my body, and we weren't in a relationship. I could nip this in the bud and move on with my life, and he'd never know.

But maybe it was the hormones, maybe it was my frazzled brain, but the thought of getting rid of this barnacle of a fetus made me sad enough to start crying again.

I'm really losing it, I thought.

"You need to go to your doctor and get this confirmed," said Naoko. "Or at least make an appointment at the clinic here on campus. Are you still on your parents' insurance? You're an adult now, but when I got my IUD last year, my mom freaked out when she got the explanation of benefits or whatever in the mail." Naoko rolled her eyes. "So much for patient confidentiality."

I definitely didn't want my family to know—at least not right this second. They'd look at me like they always did, shaking their heads and saying, *Only you, Kate.* As if I'd been stupid enough to have sex without a condom, or as if I'd done this on purpose. Nobody had reacted that way when Mari had revealed that she'd drunkenly married Liam. But Mari had been the good sister; Dani, the dutiful one.

Me? I was the naughty one. The bad one. I was smart, but that seemed to have been eclipsed by my tendency to be impulsive.

"It'll be okay." Naoko patted my arm. "If all else fails, you, me, and Henry can become a throuple and raise this baby together." Henry was Naoko's long-time boyfriend and fellow band geek. He played the saxophone and worshiped the ground Naoko walked on.

I smiled for the first time that morning. "I'd marry you both if I could."

"I know. And I'd totally be your lesbian lover if I were gay. My mom would probably die of a heart attack, though, so we'd have to keep it a mega secret."

"You sure Henry would be into it?"

Naoko waved a dismissive hand. "He'll do whatever I say, duh."

After Naoko left for her part-time barista gig, I made an appointment to see a doctor at the campus clinic. Right as I confirmed the appointment for three days from now, an email landed in my inbox from none other than my baby daddy himself.

A burst of anxiety made me start sweating, as if he'd somehow known I'd just made an appointment to confirm I was, in fact, pregnant with his baby. *Our* baby.

Wait, when had I started thinking of this thing as a baby?

The email, however, simply read:

Dear Ms. Wright,

I'd like to schedule a time to meet with you to further discuss your class schedule. I'm available in the morning Wednesday and Friday of this week. I'm happy to meet outside of my office if that's easier for you.

Best wishes,

Prof. Lochlann Gallagher, PhD.

I snorted at his formality. This man had had his dick inside my hoohah, and he wrote me an email like *that?* I was so tempted to reply with that that I had to close my laptop and return to it half an hour later after I'd calmed down.

I realized with even more irritation that I'd agreed to hang out with Dani that Friday morning, and my appointment was early on Wednesday. I'd have to meet Fancy Pants Professor Gallagher after my appointment.

Great, just great. How lucky was I?

When I replied to his email, I wrote:

Dear Professor Gallagher,

Please meet me on Wednesday at ten o'clock in the morning at The Bean Brewery on Main Street, if that is convenient for you. I do so enjoy their cinnamon latte—so scrumptious!

I look forward to our scheduled assignation.

Yours most sincerely,

Katherine Wright, B.S., 1st year materials and science student, amazing overall human

~

WHEN I EXITED the clinic three days later, I glared up at the sun. Why was it so happy and shiny? It should be raining because this damn city should always reflect my mood. It should be cold, rainy, gray, and sad.

Okay, maybe not sad—just scared. When the nurse practitioner had told me in her cheery voice that I was pregnant and that they could do an ultrasound right then to check on the fetus, I'd wanted to scream and cry.

Oh, and in case you were wondering, when the parasite is this small, you don't get to have one of those "squirt goo on your belly" ultrasounds. You get the "giant wand shoved up your vagina" type of ultrasound.

So after basically losing my virginity a second time to an ultrasound wand, I crossed the street to sit on a bench in a tiny park about a mile from campus. A few moms with their kids played on the playground; one toddler tried to climb onto a swing and subsequently face-planted into the ground. I had to cover my mouth to keep myself from laughing.

It was better than crying my eyes out for the millionth time this week.

I checked the time—nine o'clock. I still had an hour to

kill before I had to meet with my baby daddy. When I'd heard the heartbeat of our barnacle on the ultrasound, the realization that I was truly pregnant had hit me hard. I'd teared up, feeling both awed and terrified at the same time. What did I know about babies? I thought toddlers face-planting was funny. I could barely keep my succulent alive, for Christ's sake, let alone another human being.

Most of all, I knew I had to tell Lochlann. That thought alone sent a wave of anxiety crashing through me. My palms got sweaty, and I imagined all sorts of ways that conversation could go.

Scenario 1: Lochlann is overjoyed and immediately goes down on one knee to propose. I run from the cafe in horror.

Scenario 2: Lochlann bursts into tears and runs from the cafe before getting on a flight straight back to Ireland.

Scenario 3: Lochlann thinks I'm lying and refuses to listen to me. He says it's probably some other guy's baby. I then murder him.

None of those scenarios sounded appealing. And worst of all, how the hell was I going to attend grad school, further my research, and have a baby all on my own? I would be receiving a small stipend for living expenses, but certainly not enough to care for an infant. I'd have to move back in with my parents if Lochlann refused to help me. Just that thought alone made me want to melt into a sad, pathetic puddle.

I loved my parents and my sisters, but they'd never really understood me. A baby would just mean being under their roof for God knew how long.

I started walking toward the cafe when it was only five minutes until ten o'clock. I'd been so lost in thought that I'd lost track of time. I hurried down the sidewalk, almost running into an old lady walking her giant Doberman. Both dog and lady barked at me. I muttered an apology, hoping against hope that Lochlann would also be running late.

By the time I arrived, I was hot, sweaty, and frazzled. I looked around the cafe, almost breathed a sigh of relief, when I spotted a dark head of hair at a corner table. Based on his expression, he wasn't happy that I was late.

"Ms. Wright," he said as I approached. "You're late."

I'd been running—okay, more like jogging pathetically—to the point that I had to lean over and catch my breath.

"At. The. Park. Sorry. Lost. Track. Of. Time." I inhaled after each word like a fish flopping on a deck after being pulled from the water.

"Are you all right?" Lochlann took my arm and had me sit down. He began to fan me with a book he'd brought. "You're bright red."

That remark just made me blush. I tended to turn red when I was hot, like I'd gotten a sunburn.

I had not wanted Lochlann to see me again all sweaty, red, and out of breath.

"I'm fine. Sorry. Give me a second," I wheezed.

Lochlann sat down across from me and waited.

Under my lashes, I drank him in: he was wearing jeans and a sweater today. I'd never seen him dress casually. In Ireland, he'd been wearing dress pants, just like he had been when I'd met him in his office. Seeing him looking so accessible and handsome made my heart do a little happy dance in my chest.

But based on the way he was looking at me, his heart wasn't dancing. His heart probably wore the exact expression someone had when you told them you had raging diarrhea: vague disgust with a tinge of concern.

"Would you like something to drink?" Lochlann's Irish accent broke through my thoughts.

"Uh, tea. Chai, I guess."

To my surprise, he said, "I'm surprised. You seem like a coffee drinker."

"I do usually, but now…" I swallowed that remark. Yeah, I wasn't going to blurt the news that he was going to be a dad right this second.

Especially when he was still acting like he didn't recognize me. *Or he really doesn't remember you*, that evil voice inside my head whispered.

Shut the hell up, voice. I am the most memorable person in the existence of forever. And there's no way he'd forget our epic sex-a-thon.

Lochlann cleared his throat, looking uncomfortable. "I'll be right back," he muttered.

As I waited for Lochlann to return, I considered how I'd break the news to him. Did I just blurt it right out? Or did I try to ease into it? *What are your thoughts on children? Well, you're in luck—I'm having one and it's yours!*

Yeah, that'd be a terrible idea.

A cup of tea was placed in front of me. The steam curled toward my nose, and I inhaled the spicy scent gratefully.

I could do this. I could put on my big girl panties, remind Lochlann of our fling, and then give him this bombshell news.

But before I could open my mouth, he said, "I'm sure you're wondering why I asked to meet with you this morning."

"Um—isn't it about my schedule?"

"No."

I waited for him to elaborate. His dark eyes narrowed, as if I'd done something offensive. Again.

When we'd met in Ireland, Lochlann had been drinking, and I realized the alcohol had loosened him up. He'd possessed a dry humor that had immediately set my lady parts a'tingling. When he'd reached over and touched my thigh, his gaze dark with desire, I'd almost burst into flames. It hadn't taken long for us to go back to the hotel to bang each other into next Tuesday.

Where had *that* Lochlann gone? This one seemed like a shell of the man I'd met that night. Then again, booze tended to make people act differently than normal. Maybe he'd been drunker than I'd realized.

"I wanted to speak with you about our previous history," he said in the same tone you'd say *It's raining today*.

I'd just taken a sip of my tea and subsequently choked on it. Coughing, I wiped at my watering eyes as Lochlann waited for me to get a hold of myself.

"What?" I croaked.

"I made a mistake in pretending I didn't recognize you at our first meeting. I'll admit, I was so surprised I thought it was the best course of action." Lochlann folded his hands. "But again, that wasn't wise. That doesn't mean we have to make this more complicated, however."

"I don't understand."

He leaned toward me, and I caught a whiff of that scent that had driven me wild back in Ireland. "Ms. Wright. We had one night together that could put my career in jeopardy. It would behoove us to act as if it had never happened from now on." He leaned back and looked away. "I considered having you transfer to another advisor, but our research is too similar. It would raise suspicion."

He fell silent. I waited from him to apologize, or to say something less…cold.

Maybe it was my raging hormones; maybe it was the blank look on his face as he waited for me to agree to acting like our fling had been barely worth remembering. Or that this wasn't just about *him*, that if people found out we'd slept together, I'd lose the respect of my peers. I was already on shaky ground, being a woman in STEM. If people thought I'd gotten ahead by fucking my advisor?

I could never show my face in the department again.

And right then, I knew I couldn't tell him about this baby. Beyond that, I didn't know what I'd do.

I'll figure that out later.

"Well, do we have an agreement?" Lochlann sounded almost irritated.

Good. Some emotion for once.

"There's nothing new to agree on," I lied. "It was just one night, like you said. I'd already forgotten it." I looked at my fingernails, trying to sound bored.

"You seemed out of sorts at our first meeting."

"Well, it's not every day your advisor turns out to be your summer hookup."

Lochlann's lips curled upward. "Indeed."

I picked at imaginary dirt under my nails. "I already have a boyfriend. Steve. I told you about him last time, remember? So you don't have to be afraid I'll want to pick this up where we left off."

My heart was pounding, and I felt sweat break out on

my upper lip. I caught Lochlann's stormy gaze as I pounded the last nail in the coffin.

"The sex wasn't that great, anyway."

We stared at each other. Cliché, but you could've heard a pin drop. At the very least, I could've sworn I heard Lochlann's masculine pride drop and clatter on the hardwood floor.

To my surprise, Lochlann took my hand and stroked my palm with gentle fingers.

"You're a terrible liar, Kate," he murmured, heat lacing his words.

"I'm not lying."

"You won't look me in the eye."

I looked him straight in the eye and said slowly, "I'm not lying."

"I distinctly remember how you begged me to fuck you," he continued in that lazy, heated voice. "How you came all over my cock as I fucked you. How you told me how much you loved when I rubbed your clit and how you dripped onto my fingers—"

I stood up so quickly my chair tipped over. I was shaking: with arousal, with rage, with triumph. He hadn't forgotten me, the fucker.

"And now you can't touch me," I said, smiling deviously. "Have fun with that, Professor. Say a prayer you don't die of blue balls."

CHAPTER SIX

KATE

Three months earlier

I'm sure you're wondering: how did this fling happen in the first place?

Well, in June I was attending my sister Mari's wedding in Ireland. I'd never been there (no one in my family had, actually), and I'd been especially excited to meet some hot Irishmen. My soon-to-be brother-in-law, Liam, had an accent that could set a woman's panties on fire. Not that I was lusting after my sister's fiancé. Just someone with a voice and accent like his.

I never claimed I wasn't shallow, okay?

My family arrived in Dublin a week before the wedding, mostly to help Mari prepare and to play tourist. I'd gotten bored hanging around my parents, I'll admit, mostly because my dad wanted to go to all the gardens and talk plants while my mom wanted to go to any place where you could find faeries. Me, being a scientist, could only take my mom's talking about the alignment of the planets and the fae folk emerging during the full moon or whatever for so long without losing my patience.

I'd also wanted to go to Ireland to forget the fact that I'd made the waitlist for UW and was still waiting to see if they'd officially accept me. I'd taken the news as well as you'd expect—badly—when I'd gotten the email back in March. As the weeks had passed, it became less and less likely that someone would drop out and give me their spot. I'd emailed the department for an update before I'd gone to Ireland, and two days before the wedding, had gotten a reply.

No news as of yet, but we'll let you know if that changes.

So what was a morose girl to do? Go to a pub and get trashed, of course.

One of the things I could appreciate about the Irish is that they do not fuck around when it comes to their booze. Americans are pansies in comparison, let's be honest here. I wandered to a pub a few blocks from our hotel so I didn't run into anyone from the wedding party. I didn't really want to hear about how happy Mari was, or how happy Dani was with Jacob, or about anyone's happiness.

Because when you're a sad girl you want to wallow in your sadness. Other people's happiness is like throwing water onto the Wicked Witch of the West: you melt into a puddle if you get too close to it.

"Give me a pint," I said to the bartender, slapping a few euros onto the counter.

"Of what?" The bartender motioned toward the array of choices.

"Whatever is best."

The bartender muttered something that sounded like

bloody Americans before pouring some dark beer into a glass and pushing it toward me.

"I could be Canadian, you know," I said sagely.

"A Canadian would apologize for wasting my time."

I saluted him. "Touché."

I drank the dark beer, not caring what it tasted like. I just wanted the alcohol to make me forget that I was a total failure and destined to live in a tiny apartment with twenty cats.

Okay, I was being melodramatic. But I'd planned everything on getting into grad school, and I'd somehow managed to be chosen as an alternate for three programs—but no official yeses. How demoralizing. I would've thought they'd accept me because I had a vagina and these programs were hardly crawling with estrogen.

Out of the corner of my eye, I couldn't help but notice a man sitting alone at a table in the corner. He was drumming his long fingers against the wooden table, and he was wearing dark-rimmed glasses that he periodically pushed up his hawk-like nose. He had a strong jaw, and it looked like you could bounce a quarter off of it.

I licked my lips. I licked my lips a second time when I saw how his dress shirt gaped open at the collar.

Yum City.

The man, as if knowing I was gawking at him, caught my gaze. And we had a *moment.* You know, those moments where your breath catches in your chest, time stops, and your heart skips a beat?

Either I'm falling in lust or I'm having a heart attack.

The man turned away after that moment. I scowled at

him. Seriously? He wasn't even going to attempt to come over and flirt with me?

I needed a game plan. I needed—oh shit, he was coming over here right now, like I'd summoned him.

"Lady, did you hear me?"

I blinked over my shoulder at the bartender. "Uh?"

"You still owe me five euro."

I began to dig in my wallet. I'd forgotten to bring a credit card that didn't fuck me over for foreign transaction fees, so cash it was. But before I found what I needed, the man placed some coins on the counter. "Get this woman another drink, too," he said smoothly.

I looked up and found myself drowning in sexy pools of sexy male. My lady parts danced a jig. My nipples hardened. I was infinitely glad I didn't have a dick, because I'd have a boner that everyone in this pub would be able to see.

"Thank you," I said, trying to sound smooth. I tried to turn my spinning barstool back toward the counter, but I ended up spinning it too fast and almost fell off of it.

"Whoa there." The man grabbed me by the waist to steady me. "Careful there."

I let out a surprised laugh that turned into an awkward giggle. God, could I get even stranger?

It wasn't like I was a total novice when it came to men. I'd dated one guy in undergrad, and he'd squished my boobs as I'd touched his dick. But Grayson hadn't ever tried to go further, and when he'd moved to Capitol Hill—only a few miles from campus but basically a continent away in Seattle —we'd drifted apart.

Okay, fine, I was technically a virgin and my flirting skills needed work. I'd spent more time in the lab than I had working to attract a man.

Yet tonight, something shifted inside me. Or more accurately, I wanted something *new* inside me. I didn't want to be the crazy science girl tonight. I wanted to be alluring. Irresistible. Fuckable.

"These things are a total hazard," I said. "Thanks for saving me."

"You're welcome." The man's voice was pure Irish deliciousness, and I savored every word he said. Liam's accent had faded since he'd moved to the States. This man's, though, was pure Irish and I wanted to lick every one of his vowels and consonants.

Definitely don't tell him you just thought that.

"You American?" The man took a long drink of his beer.

"How can you all tell? I could be Canadian."

"Are you?"

I stuck out my lower lip. "No," I muttered into my beer, "I'm from the States." I pointed a finger at the man and added, "But I made sure to leave my fanny pack at home, you know. And I've only asked if there was a Starbucks nearby once."

"Liar."

My eyebrows shot to my hairline.

"You've asked at least three times, I'm sure."

I let out a startled laugh. Oh, he was charming, and that was dangerous. Grayson had been charming, too, but like a puppy is charming. This man? He was smooth and it was sexy as hell.

I wiped my damp palms on my jeans.

"Um, what's your name? I'm Kate." I thrust out my hand and hoped he didn't feel how clammy it had been.

He took my hand and folded it in his. "Lochlann." He took in my appearance, assessing me. "So what's an American girl doing here, drinking alone? Bad night?"

"How could you tell?"

His gaze traveled from my face to my legs, sending a burst of heat through my veins. "You aren't dressed to take a man home, for one, and until you looked over at my table, you didn't notice a single man in this pub."

"How observant of you. Or creepy."

"I come to this pub every week, and I see a lot of women." Lochlann held up a finger. "They're here with girl-friends; they're here alone, looking for a man; or they're here with their man."

"The amount of data you have on the women of this bar should freak me out, but I'm too lazy to do anything about it," I said.

"Data is always useful, yes."

"But I think you're wrong about one thing. If you haven't had enough of a sample set of my type of woman, how can you ascertain our real goal in coming here?"

Lochlann rubbed his chin. "The numbers have been limited, it's true."

"And isn't your supposing I'm not here to find a man based solely on your biased opinion that women have to dress a certain way to attract a certain type of man?"

"Not a biased opinion on that front: the women who wear little in the way of clothing generally leave with a man. Or a few men."

I rolled my eyes. "Well, you're wrong about me. I came

here specifically to find a man. But not one who cares about how I dress." I was lying through my teeth. I'd dressed in my ratty jeans and sweatshirt and had worn my favorite pair of Converse because I hadn't wanted to be bothered.

"And look, I caught your attention," I said, smirking. "So you just disproved your own point."

"Perhaps I meant to do that."

I just laughed at him. Arrogant males weren't exactly rare for me. I was used to them after spending the majority of my academic career in STEM. I'd been mansplained to so many times that I'd lost count ages ago.

"You sound like the guys I go to school with," I said, shaking my head.

"Please don't tell me you're in high school."

I batted my eyelashes at him. "I'm sorry, I'm only sixteen. Please treat me gently."

He scowled at me. "You can't buy booze here until you're eighteen. If you're going to lie, at least check your facts."

"I'm just messing with you. You look so cute when you're pissed."

He considered me for such a long moment that I had to restrain myself from squirming. It was like he saw me as some rare species he'd never encountered before.

"You're quite saucy, aren't you?" he said.

"Is that a bad thing?"

"No, but I imagine that you tend to scare away any boys who try to approach you."

"I'm going to take that as a compliment."

"You should. You don't need any boys in your life."

I snorted. "Yet here you are, talking to me."

His expression was completely serious now. "I'm not a boy. What you want is a man."

Heat coiled inside my belly, and as Lochlann gazed at me, it was like my entire body was about to combust. I was also tempted to tell him he was wrong, wrong, wrong—boys loved me. I was the most popular girl with all the boys.

Except my one boyfriend, Grayson, had told me when we'd broken up that I intimidated him.

I feel like you're always expecting more from me. It gets kind of exhausting, he'd said.

I hadn't been all that sad that we'd ended our relationship, if I were being honest.

Lochlann leaned toward me. "I don't think you were interested in any man here until you saw me, because you knew I was the perfect man for what you needed."

I almost laughed at his arrogance, but he was completely serious. If only I had the confidence of a straight, white man. I could rule the world so easily.

"You're the one who came over here," I pointed out.

"You're the one who eye-fucked me across the room."

I pursed my lips because I didn't have any response to that.

Lochlann chuckled, the sound making me want to fall into his arms like a swooning idiot. "Let's cut to the chase, Kate: I want to fuck you. I think you want to be fucked. Do you have a place in mind where we could accomplish this?"

Redness spread across my cheeks. I'd never, in my life, been spoken to like that, and it was somehow the hottest thing I'd ever heard. Shouldn't I be offended? Slap him for his audacity? Except I was practically creaming my underwear and about to tell him to fuck me over on the pool table.

If he knew I was a virgin, would he still want to sleep with me? *Doubtful.* Men didn't have one-night stands with virgins. Although that data was based solely on…absolutely no facts whatsoever.

Lochlann didn't seem perturbed that I hadn't answered yet. He merely finished his beer and watched me closely.

"You don't know anything about me," I said finally.

"I know you're beautiful." He took my hand, intertwining our fingers. "I can see how red you are, how you blush when I lean toward you. Your pupils are dilated: classic response of sexual interest. I bet if I touched your pussy, you'd be soaking wet already."

I yanked my hand from his. "You're—oh my God!"

"Tell me I'm wrong."

He wasn't, but I wasn't about to admit that. What a dickwad. I didn't care how hot he was. He could enjoy his own hand tonight for all I cared.

"Now you're upset," he said obviously. "You shouldn't be. This is all chemical. You already showed me you're a smart girl. Don't look at this with emotion. Look at it as an experiment."

"Are you seriously proposing we bang to collect *data points?*"

His smile practically lit up this dingy pub. He chucked me under the chin and slid smoothly from his own stool. "Mostly just proving that animal attraction can happen quickly and should be enjoyed, if both parties are consenting and of age. We both know you aren't sixteen, but I'd prefer not to have sex with a teenager all the same."

When he slid his hand down my back, to rest right above my ass, the anticipation of him touching me elsewhere nearly made me scream.

"I'm twenty-six," I lied. *Why am I lying* again? I must've wanted him to think I was more experienced than I was. Maybe twenty-two wasn't much better than eighteen. Maybe I was just drunk and dumb.

The uh-oh voice in my head started squawking, but I ruthlessly told it to shut the hell up.

"I'm thirty-two," he said.

"That's cool."

He smiled, waiting, stroking the small of my back.

"I have a hotel room," I breathed finally.

"Excellent."

"You can come with me to it, if you want."

"I do want that."

"Okay."

I stared up at him, completely unable to move.

"You'll either need to lead the way or tell me which hotel it is," he said gently.

"The Crown. Just up the street."

Lochlann's expression flashed with something, but he just nodded. "Then let's go."

CHAPTER SEVEN

LOCHLANN

Still three months earlier

W hen I'd first seen Kate in that pub three months
ago, I hadn't intended on approaching her. Liam
had recently got in touch with me to ask me to attend his
wedding, and I'd been a bit overwhelmed with seeing family
I'd not been around since we'd been kids.

Liam and I hadn't seen each other since he'd been a
short, skinny kid, while his sister had just been a baby. Now
his sister was in college, a young woman, while Liam was
marrying a gorgeous, intelligent woman. Lucky bastard.

That evening, I'd sat down at my usual table, nursing a
beer, when I'd seen Kate enter the pub. I'd met Liam and
Mari earlier that day, but I'd yet to meet the rest of the
wedding party. It hadn't occurred to me that Kate was
Mari's sister when I'd seen her. She didn't look much like
her: where Mari was red-haired and tall, but Kate was dark-
haired and average height.

Kate came inside the pub, laughing at something on her

phone, her hair in a braided bun on top of her head. She cooed at a patron's dog that sat at his feet and stopped to have a conversation with Barry.

Definitely an American, I thought in amusement. Besides the fact that her accent gave her away, she had that intrinsic friendliness Americans tended to project. They'd talk to anyone if given half a chance.

I watched Kate, not knowing who she was, intrigued despite myself. It wasn't as if there weren't Americans in Dublin, but they didn't usually visit pubs like these: watering holes that generally only the locals knew existed.

Kate finally sat down at the bar, speaking to the bartender. At this angle, I could see her profile: lightly tanned, with a pointed chin. She looked like some fae creature come to lead a man to her kingdom under a hill. Based on how many of the men in the pub were staring at her, she captivated men without much effort.

I hadn't come to the pub for a woman. Truth be told, I hadn't had sex in two years, not since Sophie had left me. I'd been knee-deep in research while working towards being accepted for a professor position in the States. Women hadn't crossed my mind.

Well, not usually. There were nights when I'd longed for a warm body, a wet pussy, the smell of a woman's perfume. Sometimes the loneliness got to a man. Your cat could only provide so much interaction, and jerking off with your hand could only satisfy you for so long.

The moment Kate's gaze landed on mine, though, it was like an electric shock through my body. And she didn't turn away, blushing. No, she drank me in with unabashed interest.

I want her, was the insane, immediate thought I had. And before my brain could take over, I let my intuition guide me. Or my cock. I didn't particularly care which.

"I don't usually do this," said Kate, breathless as we approached her hotel. When I'd finally taken my gaze off of her, I realized it was the same hotel Liam was staying at. My heart skipped with a burst of anxiety. Was Kate a part of the wedding party?

Then again, what were the odds? The hotel was huge: ten floors, hundreds of rooms. Kate could be on a trip abroad, or studying at university for the summer.

Kate stared up at me, the streetlights illuminating her features. With her long lashes and upturned eyes, she looked like a cat.

I touched her pointed chin. "You don't usually do what?"

"This." She waved a hand at me.

"You mean take random men up to your hotel room for a good shag?"

She blushed. "Yes. I mean, no. I don't." She seemed like she was going to say something else, but then shut her mouth.

Was she getting cold feet? If she told me to go, I would, despite my raging erection. I wasn't about to coerce a woman into sex.

"Do you want me to leave?" I offered, caressing her jaw.

She shook her head. "I'm good. Come on." Grabbing my hand, she practically dragged me inside, which made me bite back a startled laugh. It wasn't as if I was the one who needed to be persuaded.

When we arrived at Kate's door, she kept looking

around, as if somebody were going to pop out of a nearby room and chastise her. Was she here with her parents? No, she was twenty-six. She was more than old enough to travel alone.

Kate's hand was shaking as she inserted the key card and pulled it out too quickly. She kept getting the red light, and when she growled in frustration I couldn't help but laugh.

"Here, let me." I took the card from her and, in one swipe, got the door to unlock.

"Show-off," she muttered.

Kate rushed to the bed and began to toss clothes into a nearby dresser. Looking around, she had stuff everywhere: books on the desk, snacks on the nightstand, and I was pretty sure she was trying to hide her pile of dirty laundry. I had to chew on my cheek when she stuffed a pair of knickers inside a t-shirt, as if it were improper for the man she wanted to sleep with to see what she wore under her clothes.

"Sorry it's such a mess," she said, kicking something under the bed. "I wasn't expecting visitors."

"You really aren't very good at this."

She whirled on me, scowling. "I didn't have time to read the One-Night Stand Handbook, okay?"

Kate kept organizing papers, like I'd lose my erection if she didn't tidy up. It was adorable. I wrapped my arms around her waist, pulling her against me.

"Let's leave that," I rumbled, kissing her neck.

She shuddered. I could tell she was nervous, and I wanted to make her melt, to stop her busy mind from coming up with reasons why this was a bad idea.

I kissed up to her ear, nibbling on the lobe at the same

time I pushed her sweatshirt up to cup one of her breasts through her t-shirt. Her breathing quickened: a good sign. But she was still too tense. I wanted her languid. I wanted her open, and receptive, and dripping wet.

We had all night, and I intended to make it count.

Despite my failed relationship with Sophie, I'd always enjoyed giving a woman pleasure first. Making her moan, making her come, whether that was with my fingers, my mouth, or my cock. Sophie had always loved it when I'd licked her pussy with light strokes until she'd orgasm.

"What makes you come?" I said in Kate's ear. "What do you like?"

"Um." She wiggled when I rolled her nipple between my thumb and index finger. "I like what you're doing now."

Considering she was pressing her arse against my erection and not skittering away like a scared rabbit, I already knew that bit of information.

How innocent was she? She seemed so awkward and innocent that I could've almost believed she was a virgin, but she was twenty-six. I'd never known anyone who'd stayed a virgin beyond twenty, maybe twenty-two.

I slipped her out of her sweatshirt and turned her around, kissing her hard. She moaned, and when she ran her fingers through my hair, I deepened the kiss.

I slid my tongue inside her mouth. A moment later she tentatively responded, but soon that hesitation melted away.

Before I knew it, Kate was practically climbing up my body like an overstimulated squirrel. I laughed against her lips.

"We have all night," I said, breaking the kiss.

"I feel like I've been waiting forever."

Why did I get that same feeling for a woman I'd only just met? As if afraid of my own emotions, I turned her around so I couldn't see her face. I stripped her of her t-shirt and unhooked her bra, sucking on the side of her neck as I pulled on her nipples. She moaned and arched against me.

Blood pooled in my already hardened cock. Stepping back, I took in the curve of her spine, the pale skin of her lower back, the smattering of freckles on her shoulder blades. I could make out a faint tan line from her bathing suit.

"Turn around," I said.

Kate had put her hands over her breasts, but as she turned she took them down. Her tits were small but perky, the nipples puffy.

"Get on the bed." I began to undress myself.

"Why do you sound like you're going to tie me up and whip me?"

I chuckled. "Do I look like the kind of guy who carries around a whip with him?"

"Dunno. You could be packing something extra in those pants for all I know." She arched an eyebrow.

I took her hands, pressing them to my cock. "Does that seem like I'm carrying something extra?"

"No. It doesn't."

"Get on the bed, Kate."

She got on the bed. I almost ripped my clothes in my haste to get them off. Soon I was down to my pants, Kate having stripped out of her jeans to show off her knickers. Knickers that had some cartoon characters all over them.

"Oh my God." She groaned as she realized what was she wearing. "I'd totally forgotten I'd worn these today."

I pulled at the wide elastic band. "They're charming. What even are they, though?"

She looked at me in surprise. "They're Rick and Morty." When I gave her a blank look, she added, "From the show, *Rick and Morty?*"

"Sorry, never heard of it."

She sighed deeply, clearly disappointed in my lack of interest in recent animated programs. "That is so sad. It's only the best cartoon ever," she said.

"I'll take that under advisement," I said as seriously as I could.

She then wrinkled her nose. "But if I'd known this was going to happen I would've worn a thong. Or nothing at all." She sighed, collapsing back onto the bed. "Now you're going to remember me as the girl wearing Rick and Morty underpants."

"You know there's a solution to this problem, right?"

She looked up at me hopefully.

I hooked my fingers in the waistband and subsequently yanked them down her legs, tossing the offending knickers into some dark corner of the hotel room.

"There. Rick and Morty have been defeated," I said proudly.

"I love how you say Rick and Morty. It sounds way too sexy. Rick and Morty shouldn't be sexy; I'm a little creeped out, honestly."

I had a feeling Kate chattered when she was nervous. I placed my hands next to her head, looming over her, before widening her legs with my knees to make room for me.

"All right?" I said, hovering above her.

She nodded before taking my face in her hands and drawing me down for a kiss.

It was as if the kiss ignited another fire within us. Soon we were kissing hard and deeply, my stubble scraping against her cheeks. Teeth clacked; tongues slicked together. Kate's hands were busy, feeling my chest and sides. When she found a ticklish spot, she laughed and tried to tickle me further.

"Not happening," I growled, pinning her to the bed. "Be a good girl and let me have my wicked way with you."

"Now you sound hella fucking sexy."

I preened under her words. It had been a long time since a woman had told me that. In the recent years, any compliments I'd got were about my research. Clurichaun got more compliments from people who saw him lounging in the living room window.

I kissed and licked my way down Kate's torso, stopping to admire her breasts. When I sucked a nipple into my mouth, she gasped and arched in surprise. Once again I wondered how much experience she had. Had no man played with her like this? Had they just stuck their cocks in, pumped a few times, and that was that?

I kissed the underside of her breast. "You smell like cherries," I said wonderingly.

"Oh no, you've found out my secret: I rub cherries all over my boobs in the morning just in case."

I snorted, tweaking the other nipple. "Don't be impertinent."

"I'd agree if, again, you didn't sound so sexy."

Fine, I'd take the compliment. Besides, I'd have her writhing and screaming soon enough. I parted her thighs, slicking a finger through her pussy. She was already soaking wet, and when my finger just circled her clit, she moaned.

"How do you touch yourself?" I whispered as I turned her onto her side, her left leg hitched onto my hip. "Tell me."

Kate shuddered. "Harder—yes, no, wait—"

I laughed as I moved my finger around the hood of her clit, not touching the straining bundle of nerves directly. "Here? Like this?"

"Um." She let me rub before she took my hand and moved it all of a millimeter. "There. Oh, harder. Yes, like that..."

Her entire body tightened as I followed her instructions. As she moaned and writhed, I began to rub her clit harder at the same time I sucked on one of those cherry-flavored nipples of hers. Soon the only sounds in the room were her moans and the sound of her juicy pussy. I could feel her dripping onto my hand, and I wanted to taste every drop of her after she came.

"I'm going to come," she announced, her expression surprised. "Holy shit."

The next second, she came, her entire body shaking. I had to push her leg on my hip down to keep her from rolling away from me. I laughed softly at her continued look of shock.

"Have you never orgasmed before?" I couldn't help but ask.

"No, I have, just not with anyone else doing it." She sighed languidly. "Well, I'm beat. Good night."

I trailed my hand up her torso—the one still wet from her pussy—making sure to circle both of her nipples.

"I think you really, really needed to come." I tilted her chin up so she was looking me in the face. Sucking each of my fingers into my mouth, I tasted her tartness. If I wasn't so desperate to plunge my cock into her I'd eat her out until she screamed.

"Shit, that's hot." Kate took my hand and, to my surprise, tasted herself on my fingers. Her slick, warm tongue made me imagine it on my cock, and Christ, I needed her. Right this minute.

I rolled from the bed to grab my wallet from my trousers, Kate making a squawk of annoyance. "Are you leaving?" she complained.

I held up the foil packet. "I'm assuming you don't have your own box of condoms?"

"Oh, right. Good idea. I'm not on birth control, plus you could have the clap or something."

After I'd rolled the latex onto my cock, I kicked her legs apart and settled between them. "Just what every man wants to hear as he fucks a woman."

Kate was about to reply, but when I notched the head of my cock at her entrance and slid inside, her words were swallowed by her moan. Fuck, she was tight. The condom was the only thing keeping me from blowing my load like a teenage boy.

When Kate grimaced, I stopped. Had I hurt her? She was more than wet enough, but maybe I took things too fast. "All right?"

She inhaled deeply, then nodded. "Yes. It's good." She squinted at me. "Why did you stop?"

I laughed with a shake of my head. I began to move slowly, watching Kate's face. Her pupils were blown, her breathing increasing with each thrust. I began to increase the tempo, her pussy somehow getting wetter with each plunge of my cock inside her.

"You love my cock inside you. I can feel you, soaking it," I said.

Kate nodded. "I do love it. I didn't know if I would." She raised her hips, her rhythm awkward but her enthusiasm infectious.

Soon I began to fuck her in earnest, chasing my own orgasm. Kate pulled my head down for a wet, messy kiss. I plunged inside her, over and over, the sound of it only heightening the eroticism of the moment. The headboard bounced against the wall. The people next door surely could hear us, but I didn't care. I didn't care if the entire city of Dublin heard us: I was too far gone in the tightest pussy I'd ever experienced, inside this sassy but inexplicably innocent seductress.

Kate reached down to rub her clit, which made me smile. When her eyes rolled back inside her head, her pussy tightened around my cock at the same time. That was all it took. I came in endless spurts, practically emptying my bollocks inside the condom. It took all of my effort not to collapse on top of her.

When I pulled off the condom, there was blood on it. At first I assumed she'd started her period, but then I remembered how she'd reacted when I'd first pushed inside her.

Kate had her eyes closed, lying on her side. "Kate," I said. "Were you a virgin?"

Her eyes flew open. She then noticed the bloody condom in my hand and the blood drained from her face.

My stomach clenched. Why hadn't she told me? I should've been gentler with her. What if I'd really hurt her?

"I think I deserve an explanation," I said after I'd got rid of the condom.

Kate had wrapped a blanket around her shoulders. "Um, does it matter? I was a virgin, now I'm not. It's not a big deal."

I looked at her incredulously. "Of course it's a big deal! I could've injured you."

"You know, it's a bit of a myth that losing your virginity is this whole ordeal. I'm surprised I bled at all. It's not like I've never stuck anything up there before."

I just gave her an annoyed look.

She let out a sigh. "Okay, fine, I should've said something. But be honest: would you have slept with me if you'd known?"

"Of course not."

"Well, there's your answer."

I pulled the bedding down and had her get under the blankets, since the single one she had around her shoulders wasn't nearly thick enough.

I'd never taken anyone's virginity before, and I had to admit, I felt a strange mixture of horror and...possessiveness? That made no sense. Kate wasn't mine, and she hadn't been mine to claim like some caveman.

"Why me?" I said into the darkness. The real question I wanted to ask her was *how were you still a virgin at twenty-six?*

She shrugged one shoulder. "You're hot, and you were down to fuck. So here we are."

"Your flippancy suggests otherwise."

Kate inhaled deeply. "Okay, you want the truth?" She

turned to face me. "I'd never let myself get this close to a guy, but tonight I wanted to do something different. You were right: I needed a man, not a boy."

I brushed a few strands of hair from her face. "Then I'm honored you chose me."

When she smiled, I couldn't stop myself from kissing her once again.

CHAPTER EIGHT

LOCHLANN

Present day

After Kate—no, Ms. Wright, I had to remember that —left, I sat staring at my cold tea in utter consternation.

She'd got one over me. I had to admit that one. I'd thrown down the gauntlet. She'd taken it up and had promptly shoved it up my arse. So much for getting control of the situation.

I rubbed my temples, feeling a headache forming. Despite my irritation, I couldn't help but be impressed. I'd seen flashes of this Kate when we'd hooked up in Ireland, but apparently when she got her back up she was ruthless.

And fuck me if that wasn't sexy.

My cock hardened—all right, it was already hard from our conversation. Memories flooded my mind. I'd tried so hard to tell myself that our fling had been nothing. It had been fun, but it hadn't affected me—or so I'd told myself.

Except this girl had haunted my dreams for months now.

It was as if she'd infected me with a virus. She was the emotional equivalent of herpes. You could deal with symptoms, but it'd never go away.

One thing I knew for certain: I had to get her far away from me. I couldn't be her advisor. I was smart enough to admit to myself that I'd have her on my desk, her jeans around her ankles, and my cock inside that sweet pussy before she'd said, "Good morning, Professor."

Rifling through my briefcase, I pulled out the note that Dr. Martin had written her phone number on. And before I could rethink my decision, I called and asked her if we could meet to discuss something in my office within the next three days.

Dr. Martin asked if we could meet off campus. "It's easier for me since I live on the east side," she said. "How about we meet in Capitol Hill? Get that drink finally?"

If I had to pay for a steak dinner to get Dr. Martin to agree to this, I'd do it. So the next evening, I met up with Dr. Martin at a whiskey bar. Twenty-somethings filled the place, from scarf-wearing hipsters to kids who looked something straight out of an episode of *Friends*. One girl wore a short plaid skirt with white stockings and a choker around her neck.

When had I got so fucking old? I grumbled inwardly. I was only thirty-two, for the love of Christ.

"Lochlann!" Dr. Martin waved at me from a booth in the back. "Hi!"

I plastered a smile on my face. I needed to be charming. Charismatic. I couldn't be surly, and I couldn't demand that Dr. Martin do what I want. Too bad, really. Liam would've been better suited for this meeting. He could charm the pants off any woman.

"I'm so glad you called me," gushed Dr. Martin. Wearing a bright red dress that outlined her breasts, her hair tumbling down her shoulders, she was a knockout. She smelled like jasmine and sex appeal. When she got up from the booth to give me a friendly hug, I should've been elated.

Except...she did nothing for me. Absolutely nothing. I had to restrain a growl at my own useless libido. A relationship with a fellow professor wasn't ideal, but it was hardly on the same level as sleeping with a student.

You didn't know she was going to be your student. And you're giving her to Dr. Martin to put this entire thing to rest.

"I appreciate you meeting with me on such short notice, Dr. Martin," I said.

She waved a hand. "Call me Liz. And of course. I'm always happy to help a colleague. You were missed at happy hour this week. We need to get you to come out with all of us."

I grunted. It wasn't that I didn't like my colleagues, but when socializing drained your energy you had to be circumspect who you spent time with. Besides, I had a few more important things on my plate than drinking with my fellow professors.

"I wanted to talk to you about a student of mine. Kate Wright. I'd like you to take her on."

Dr. Martin—no, *Liz*, I reminded myself—blinked at me, her blue eyes wide. She then let out a startled laugh. "Well, this is a surprise. You sounded so sure you wanted to work with her the last time we spoke."

"Circumstances have changed."

I ordered a glass of whiskey for myself; Liz had already ordered before I'd arrived. She stared into the amber liquid, her eyebrows furrowed.

"I can't take on an additional student. I'm already at maximum capacity," she said finally.

"We can trade students."

Liz wrinkled her nose. "And force one of mine to start over with a new advisor?"

"The quarter hasn't even started yet."

"Of course, but that hardly seems fair. Besides, Kate's research is so close to yours that it wouldn't make much sense for me to advise her. As you said to me, if I remember correctly."

My jaw was clenched, and I forced myself to relax. I couldn't show how important this was to me. Not just important: absolutely crucial. If I had to continue to advise Kate, I knew in my gut that my entire career, my work visa, everything, would be utterly fucked.

"I did say that, but I believe Kate would work better with a female professor." I cleared my throat, feeling like a total sod for lying as I explained, "She doesn't much care for what I have to say. She essentially hinted that she didn't much trust male professors."

"Well, considering all of the misogyny that's rampant in STEM..." Liz sipped her whiskey. "But are you saying that you've done something inappropriate for her to feel like this?"

My stomach tightened. I couldn't tell based on Liz's expression if she was just curious or truly suspicious.

"Nothing's happened. Kate simply prefers female guidance, that's all. I thought I'd accommodate that need as best I could."

"So you're just going to pawn her off on me while upending another student's schedule and research? That hardly seems fair."

Dammit, I couldn't disagree with her. I thought hurriedly, trying to come up with some reasoning to convince Liz to trade students with me.

"I'd prefer to speak to Kate directly," added Liz, "to see how she feels about this. This is her career—not yours."

You have no fucking idea.

"I wanted to see how you'd feel about it first. I've already spoken to Kate about it." *Lies, lies, lies.*

Liz pushed her hair over her shoulder, trailing her fingers through the blonde strands. "I guess I'm not entirely certain what I'd get out of this," she said calmly, her blue eyes no longer flirtatious. "This seems like a shitty deal for me."

"Because we both have the same goals: to teach our students the best ways we can."

"Yes, but this seems like you're trying to get rid of a problem, Dr. Gallagher. Why is that?" Her red lips turned upwards into a smile. "Why give me one of the brightest students of the incoming class? Are you truly that altruistic?"

"This is about making Kate comfortable: nothing else. That should be something you'd automatically support."

I could see that that arrow had hit its mark. Liz's smile dampened, and her eyes flashed fire. "If you agree to something I want, I'll consider your proposal."

My knuckles turned white around my whiskey glass. "So a quid pro quo arrangement?"

"Exactly." Liz leaned towards me, her cleavage once again on display. "Tell me the exact reason why you want me to take Kate on as a student. That's my condition."

"Considering I already did that, I don't know how else to get you to agree."

She sighed. "Then I guess you'll just have to suffer." Liz tipped back the rest of her whiskey and stood up. "A little tip for you: when you want to make a deal, you should make sure it's worth something to both parties. Not just for you."

I scowled at her. "I'll keep that in mind," I said, my voice laced with sarcasm.

I wasn't one to threaten women—or anyone, for that matter—but the smug expression on her face rankled to the point that I stopped her from leaving to say, "I don't know what your game is, but whatever it is you aren't going to succeed."

"How many times has a man told me that in my life?" She patted my forearm. "Keep telling yourself that at night, if it makes you feel better."

"I'm not the one trying to blackmail a colleague."

"Blackmail? That's a harsh word. I was looking for a deal that benefits us both. Nothing wrong with that, is there?"

I took a deep breath and said in a low voice, "What *do* you want?"

Liz considered me, her head cocked to the side. "You really are desperate, aren't you? How about this: I'll take on Kate and give you one of my students. In exchange, I want details of your research."

I reared back. I'd been convinced she'd simply wanted me to take her out on a date. "You want credit for my work? No fucking way."

"Not credit so much as information."

I looked at her more closely, racking my brain. I remembered hearing someone in the department say that Liz was up for tenure this year, but did she have the research credentials to get it? Had she shown the university they should offer her tenure? Based on this conversation, she felt like she was on thin ice and would do anything to get off it.

"I'll think about it," I said finally, hating myself for even saying those words.

"Excellent. Call me when you make up your mind, but you should know: I won't be waiting forever."

After Liz left, I sat in the booth and stewed. Somehow the answer to my problems had only worsened the problem, and now this hole I'd dug was only getting deeper. I ordered another glass of whiskey, downing it in almost one gulp. The liquor burned my throat and gut, but it was better than feeling this expanding anxiety.

My only consolation was that both Liz and I wanted something enough that we had leverage over the other person. That would give us both a reason to keep our mouths shut—for now.

CHAPTER NINE

KATE

I stared at my sad glass of water and scowled. "Why did I agree to go to a bar with you tonight? When I can't even drink?"

"Because if I had to listen to you crying at some Hallmark romcom for the thousandth time, I was going to lose it." Naoko, dressed in a short blue romper with her hair in twin buns, kept catching looks from most of the men at the bar. But Naoko being Naoko, she didn't even notice the stares. It'd be annoying if she weren't so charming.

"I wasn't crying," I shot back. "Well, except for that one about the dog. Naoko, the dog ran away and they couldn't find it." Tears pooled in my eyes. *Damn hormones.* "And then the little boy found him because he knew the dog would always come if he heard his voice—"

"Oh my God, stop. Please don't start crying in the middle of the bar." Despite her words, Naoko squeezed my hand. "Even though you can't get wasted, we're still having fun. And then we're going to play some video games. I heard they just got in a new Pac-Man game and I know you live for Pac-Man."

"I prefer Ms. Pac-Man."

Naoko pursed her lips. "I guess pregnancy would make me a lesbian, too."

I snorted, my tears evaporating. At least for the time being. It had been a few days since I'd met with Lochlann and had that ever so *enlightening* discussion with him. I'd considered being a total creep and finding out his address to go throw something at him. Rotten fruit, dog poop, my used pregnancy tests.

He'd had the nerve to act like only his life was in trouble here. He hadn't cared a bit about me: it was all about his reputation, his career. Of course, he had no idea about the fetus-zygote-embryo growing inside me right this second. I placed a hand over my stomach, as if I'd be able to feel it when it was currently the size of a plum.

(Was it weird that I was craving plums at the moment? Did that mean I actually wanted to eat my baby?)

I wouldn't be able to hide this pregnancy for much longer. Even though I practically owned stock in the baggy sweatshirt department, people would probably notice when I came waddling into class with a huge belly come February.

"You're seriously not going to tell him?" said Naoko, breaking my thoughts, her gaze on my hand over my stomach.

"No. Maybe." I sighed. "I don't know."

When I'd arrived back at our apartment after my meeting with Lochlann, I'd been so steamed that I'd told Naoko about our conversation, although I'd left out the less savory details. She didn't need to know Lochlann had talked about how I'd come all over his fingers. Some things were TMI, even for me.

"It's not that I don't think I need to, I just don't know how to do it."

Right then, Naoko's boyfriend Henry came over to sit with us. Tall and almost gangly, Henry had a tendency to bump into things all the time. I'd seem him trip over his own feet more than once. He was like a puppy dog who had yet to figure out how his own limbs worked. It was endearing, although I'd always wondered if sex with him involved a lot of elbows in the face.

"You don't know how to do what?" asked Henry. "Don't you know everything?"

I stuck out my tongue. Henry was a bit like the older brother I'd never had. Whereas he planned every moment of his life and found great pleasure in alphabetizing his comics, I was more of a fly-by-the-seat-of-your-pants kind of gal with a side of overconfidence in my ability to accomplish tasks.

"I've never said I know everything," I countered.

"I'm pretty sure your exact words a few weeks ago were, 'I know everything and you know nothing.'"

"I was talking about the theme that existence is pointless in *Rick and Morty*. Not everything ever in the history of forever."

"I'm pretty sure you meant everything ever in the history of forever."

"Okay, you guys, cool it." Naoko took Henry's arm, patting his skinny chest. "How was sax practice, babe?"

"My favorite reed finally cracked so I had to use a new one." Henry sighed. "I hate having to use a new reed."

"Yeah, but you get to suck on a new piece of wood," I said.

Naoko kicked me under the table. Henry, lost in thought about his saxophone troubles, didn't even hear me.

I'd made Naoko swear on pain of death not to tell Henry about this whole Lochlann situation, including my pregnancy. Henry was a good guy, but he was terrible at keeping secrets. He'd blab to one of his saxophone friends and then I'd be screwed—more than I already was.

Although Henry considered himself to be more of a musician, he'd initially entered college as an engineering major. Mostly to appease his parents. When he'd subse-quently switched to being a musical education major, his mom and dad had only spoken to him through his brother for six months straight. One time his brother had even tried to give me a message for Henry when Naoko had been out of town. He'd stopped by the apartment like some weirdo who didn't know the Internet existed. Suffice to say we'd all been relieved when Henry's parents had finally decided to speak with him again like normal people.

"So how's the research going?" said Henry to me as he stole some French fries. He stuffed them into his mouth and I was fairly certain he didn't even chew them before swallowing.

"Babe, you're going to choke if you eat so fast," said Naoko.

"You look like a human vacuum cleaner," was my comment.

Henry just threw some more fries into his wide, gaping mouth. "If you didn't want me to eat your food, you shouldn't have invited me out."

I snorted. "*I* didn't invite you, and those are my fries."

"Who's your advisor again? I feel like you told me, but I have the attention span of a squirrel." Henry sighed. "I misplaced my sheet music yesterday. I eventually found it in the fridge."

"How did it get in the fridge?" said Naoko.

Henry shrugged. "No idea." He looked at me and added, "I had a huge crush on Dr. Martin. She's so hot. Please tell me you have her, Kate."

"Wait, are you *my* boyfriend or not?" Naoko flicked Henry's ear, which he hated. He squawked, giving me time to collect my thoughts.

"Her advisor is a new professor," said Naoko a moment later. "You wouldn't know him."

"A new one? Who?" Henry pulled at his now reddened ear.

"No, I have Dr. Gallagher. He's from Ireland and he was just hired." I tried to sound as nonchalant as possible, like Lochlann was a sixty-five-year-old professor with a love for tweed and hot cups of tea when his joints ached. But then again, Lochlann would probably look smoking hot in a tweed jacket with elbow patches.

"Oh, you know what," said Henry, "I heard Jamie talking to Marianne about him. She said she'd 'hit it like the fist of an angry god.' Which I'm assuming means he's hot. Is he hot?"

Naoko rolled her eyes and mouthed *sorry* to me.

"Why, do you want to date him?" I countered.

"Don't know anything about him. Besides, even if dudes were my thing, Naoko would lock me up in her basement if I tried to leave her."

"I don't even have a basement, you weirdo," said Naoko.

Luckily, Naoko and Henry playfully bickered, letting me off the hook in terms of describing how hot Lochlann was. It didn't surprise me that other students were slavering over him, though. Not only did he have an Irish accent, he was handsome and brilliant. He was like the jackpot of men. If I didn't hate him so much, I'd consider myself fortunate to have gotten him as my advisor.

But the little parasite inside me only served to remind me that nothing about my situation was fortunate at the moment.

As the evening progressed, the bar became more packed with students. It had been a warm day, especially for Seattle, and the lack of air conditioning made the air stagnant and humid. Sweat beaded on my forehead and upper lip. As I finished my second glass of water, my stomach lurched.

Shit, I did not want to puke in this dive bar's janky bathroom. I'd probably get hepatitis from the toilet seat.

I must've turned pale, because Naoko said, "Are you okay?"

"I just need to pee." When I stepped off the high barstool, my vision blurred, but I was able to grab on to the edge of the table to steady myself.

"Kate? Are you okay?" Henry was peering closely at me.

"Sorry, yeah, I'm fine. I just got down too fast." I stepped away, my vision clearing but my stomach about to revolt. The turkey sandwich I'd eaten two hours ago was threatening to make an appearance right here in the middle of the bar.

I pushed my way through the crowd. It was so loud and crowded that it felt like an eternity before I reached the bathroom in the back. I was sweating bullets at this point, and when my vision blurred, I had to lean against the wall to keep myself from falling over.

"Ms. Wright," said a voice that was from both my dreams and my nightmares.

Lochlann stood before me, tall and imperious, wearing a pair of glasses that only served to make his nose more hawk-like. It didn't help that he looked super judgy gazing down at me, as if my mere presence offended him. He then looked me up and down and scowled.

"You're rat-arsed," he said.

I squinted up at him. "Excuse me?"

"Smashed. Drunk." He wrinkled his oh-so-imperious nose. "Are you here alone?"

Christ, he thought I was drunk, when I was just about to puke my guts up because his swimmers were overly ambitious. I tried to push past him, but, to my consternation, he stopped me.

"Are you here alone?" he repeated.

I was the one to scowl now. "Why do you care? I don't have to tell you anything."

"Getting drunk alone? You know better than that."

"Do I? Isn't that how we met in the first place? You didn't seem too upset when you saw me alone at that bar in Dublin."

We stared at each other, the tension only increasing. I was now so pissed at him that I'd almost forgotten my rolling stomach—almost being the operative word here.

"You weren't drunk then," he countered. "Not like this."

Right then, my stomach heaved. But worse, I felt my vision blurring again. Either I was going to puke, faint, or just die. I hoped it was the third option. Death seemed a better option than vomiting on Lochlann's shoes or fainting like a damsel in distress.

Lochlann seemed to sense something was wrong because his expression turned concerned. "Kate, are you all right?"

I was about to say something, but before my lips could form the words my vision turned black before I fainted in Lochlann's arms.

CHAPTER TEN

LOCHLANN

I stared at the cold, white tile of the hospital, waiting for news about Kate. When she'd collapsed into my arms, her face as white as a ghost, fear like none other had gripped me. I'd laid her down on the sticky floor of the bar, yelling something about calling for an ambulance. My brain couldn't come up with the emergency number for here in the States; the only numbers I could think of were 999 or 112, both Irish numbers.

A few seconds later, Kate had opened her eyes, only to vomit profusely. I'd helped her sit up so she didn't aspirate, something a buddy of mine in college had done when he'd got so rat-arsed that he'd inhaled his own vomit and had got pneumonia as a result.

I tapped my foot on the hospital floor, rubbing my hands together. Kate's two friends, one of whom had found us and had dialed for an ambulance, sat across from me. If they were confused as to why Kate's advisor was waiting around for her in the hospital they could stay confused. I wasn't about to go home and not find out what was wrong with her.

It might be overkill to bring her to the ER, but it was better safe than sorry.

Naoko and Henry had tried to go back with Kate, but Kate had been conscious enough to tell them to stay in the waiting room for now. *You don't need to see me naked,* she'd joked.

She hadn't looked at me

The boy—Henry was his name, which he'd told me when I'd demanded to know how they knew Kate—kept glancing at me. His girlfriend, Naoko, was typing away on her phone.

"Should we call her parents?" said Henry to no one in particular.

"I don't have their number," said Naoko. "I guess I could message them on Facebook."

"She's not a minor." My tone was sharper than I'd intended, and I softened it a bit as I added, "I imagine Kate —Ms. Wright—would prefer we ask her first before messaging them."

Naoko's forehead crinkled, which made me think she disagreed with me. It wasn't that I didn't want Kate's family to come, but what was the point of distressing them when we didn't know yet what was wrong?

You're not her family either, my mind whispered.

She'd fainted right in front of me. Only a heartless bastard would leave at this point. That was at least what I told myself to justify me sitting around and waiting in this ER.

A number of people had come and gone through the automatic doors: a lot of students, given how close the hospital was to campus, but some were older folks, some were parents with children. An infant cried fitfully in its mother's arms, the mother shushing it every few seconds.

"Did you know that you have to pay mileage when you take an ambulance?" said Henry, stretching his gangly legs.

Taken aback, I said, "Are you bloody serious?" I knew the States had fucked-up healthcare, but it hadn't crossed my mind that Kate might be hit with a huge bill for this ER visit when I'd demanded someone call an ambulance.

Both Naoko and Henry blinked at my harsh tone. Henry finally said, "Yeah. Happened when I broke my arm last year and had to call 911. They charge you for the ride and the mileage."

"That's terrible," said Naoko.

Henry nodded. "Good thing this place was so close to the bar."

Too worried about Kate, I pushed aside the anxiety that filled me listening to Henry. I didn't need another thing to add to this terror building inside me. If Kate were truly sick, if she ended up in the hospital for days, if she were diagnosed with some serious condition...

An hour passed with no update, despite Naoko going up to the check-in desk to ask if someone could speak with us. I considered simply going back and finding Kate, but she'd tell me to get lost. I couldn't blame her; I'd been an absolute gobshite to her the last time we'd met.

When Naoko and Henry went in search of a vending machine, a nurse finally came out to speak with us. "I'm sorry it's taken this long," she said, her expression clearly harried. "It's been a crazy night already. Are you a relation of Ms. Wright?"

"Yes," I lied, because I wanted to know her condition

and I knew I'd never get to see her otherwise. "I'm her boyfriend," I added. *Please let her friends get lost in the hospital...*

"Oh, well, she's doing all right. She vomited a second time, but we're giving her fluids and an anti-nausea medication that's helping. The ultrasound tech will be here to check on the fetus, but we're pretty sure she just got herself dehydrated."

I didn't hear a word after the nurse said *fetus.* Kate was pregnant? How far along was she?

"You can go see her," the nurse said, looking at me strangely before she went to speak with another family.

I sat down heavily, my head about to explode from this piece of news. It must be her boyfriend's baby—the boyfriend I'd assumed she'd made up. Steve, that was his name. The guy who made lasagna.

When Naoko and Henry returned with their sodas and some candy, Henry handed me a can of seltzer. "I should've asked what you wanted, but it's better than nothing."

I smiled gamely. "Thanks."

"Any news?" said Naoko.

"Does Kate have a boyfriend?" I said, feeling my heart thump heavily inside my chest.

Henry laughed. "Kate? No way. She's super single." When Naoko elbowed him, he yelped. "What? She's the one who always says that!"

Naoko gave me a weird look before staring at her feet. "I'm not sure that's really something you need to know about."

"The nurse asked me. I didn't know the answer. Kate had mentioned a guy named Steve when we'd met, but I didn't know about their relationship." More lies. My

Catholic mam would've beat my arse if she'd heard how many lies I'd told tonight.

"Steve?" Henry's nose wrinkled. "The only Steve I know is Steve Winkler. Pretty sure he's gay, though. He plays the flute."

"What does him playing the flute have to do with his sexual orientation?" was my question.

Henry shrugged. "Never met a straight flautist, and I've known a lot."

"I'm sure Kate knows people you don't know," interjected Naoko.

"Not true. We're her only friends, unless there's a Steve in the materials department. Could be one of the incoming students." Henry pulled out his phone, now on the hunt for this Steve person.

Henry's mouth pulled into an O of surprise. "No, not that Steve. No, too old. No, too young. Oh wait, he's an engineering student." Henry showed me his phone, showing me the Instagram account of this Steve.

The photos ranged from blurry shots of birds to clearer shots of more birds. A ridiculous amount of birds. There was one photo of Steve, a giant macaw on his shoulder, Steve kissing the bird's beak. The caption read *My best girl.*

"I think he already has a girlfriend," I said wryly before I handed Henry his phone back.

"Hey, you never know. If he's in the engineering department, maybe they hooked up." Henry showed Naoko the profile. "He seems like somebody Kate would have sex with, doncha think?"

"Oh my God, we are not having this conversation," hissed Naoko.

88

"We have to solve this mystery. If Kate said she was dating someone to Dr. Gallagher, then she must be dating somebody. She's a terrible liar," said Henry.

Henry proceeded to show me more Steve profiles: one Steve was shaved bald and seemed to have an affinity for large knives; another was clearly engaged to another woman; another looked like he was all of fifteen.

Finally, after the fifth profile, I said, "Enough. This is pointless."

Henry deflated a little. Naoko rubbed his arm and whispered something into his ear. I had to admit, Henry's attempt to play detective had distracted me almost enough to forget the nurse's revelation earlier. But when silence fell, I was completely gobsmacked.

If Kate's best friends didn't know about her boyfriend, my hunch that she'd made him up just to make me jealous seemed to hold water.

Which meant that she could be pregnant with *my* baby.

When I was a kid, I went swimming in a river not far from my parents' house. We'd been warned that the current in the river was faster than it seemed, but some of my friends had dared me to swim across it. Being all of seven, I'd thought I was invincible. I'd been able to swim about halfway when the current had caught at me. Soon I was tumbled underwater. It was only sheer luck that I'd been able to grab onto a nearby rock and avoid drowning.

My mam was still mad at me for that stunt, even decades later.

But that feeling, of the water closing in, my lungs desperate for air, was the same sensation I felt right now. Had a one-night stand really resulted in a pregnancy? But

I'd worn a condom. Had it been old? I thought back to when I'd put it in my wallet and couldn't remember. Wouldn't I have noticed if I'd come inside her, though?

"We're going back to see her. You want to come?" said Naoko quietly.

"I'll wait."

I didn't want to have this confrontation with Kate's friends present. Assuming Kate had got pregnant after our fling in June, she was almost past her first trimester. That meant she had to have already known she was pregnant.

It also meant that she hadn't told me. Had she ever intended to tell me?

I clenched my fists, trying to swallow the anger that threatened to overwhelm me. I forced myself to calm down. I didn't know if this even was my baby.

I knew that, and yet something deep inside me told me it was.

A little later, Naoko and Henry had to go home. They both gave me awkward glances, like they didn't know what to do with me.

"Kate said we could go home since she doesn't know when she'll be discharged," explained Naoko. She had a guilty expression on her face. "I still hate to leave her."

"She wanted us to go home," said Henry. "Besides, she's just going to sleep."

"I know, I know." Naoko said to me, "You can go home too, if you want."

"I will in a bit. You two go on."

They hesitated for a second before finally leaving. Good. I couldn't wait another day to speak with Kate, but I didn't need her friends hovering.

When I entered the large room that housed two other beds, the same nurse from before directed me to Kate's room, which was really just a space partitioned off from the other patients. The smell of antiseptic filled my nose. I heard a man speaking behind the partition, something about how he did not want to "piss in a cup right now."

Kate had her eyes closed. She looked so small and fragile, lying in that hospital bed. She had an IV hooked up to her arm. I looked at her abdomen, as if I could somehow see the baby inside her now. But she was covered in blankets, so if she had a bump, there was no way I could see it right now.

I stepped towards the bed, my emotions a mix of concern and anger. The words I'd had on my tongue had evaporated.

"Naoko, I told you to go home," mumbled Kate, her eyes still closed.

"I'm not Naoko," I said.

Kate's eyes flew open. When she saw my expression, her eyes just widened.

"So, tell me," I said quietly, "is the baby mine? And if it is, were you ever going to tell me?"

CHAPTER ELEVEN

KATE

Seeing Lochlann standing over me, his eyes hard and his jaw clenched, I wanted to throw myself under the bed and hide like a little kid. Instead, I was so startled that I yanked on my arm that had the IV in it, making the machine start beeping in warning.

"What the hell?" I tried moving the IV stand, but it only kept beeping.

"Unfold your arm," said Lochlann, tapping on my forearm.

I'd bent my arm in half, the IV line in the crook of my elbow. The nurse hadn't been able to get a line into my wrist, citing that I had tiny veins that didn't like needles. I hesitated at Lochlann's command, and he sighed.

"The line is kinked," he explained. He took my arm and straightened it, and the machine finally decided it was going to shut up.

Right then, a nurse came in. "I heard beeping. Everything okay?" She checked my IV and turned to me. "You're looking a bit better, dear. How are you feeling? Any more nausea?"

I blushed, wishing Lochlann would go away. "It's better."

"Good. I'll come and check on you in a bit. You should get to go home soon."

After the nurse left, I fiddled with the paper bracelet they'd given me when I'd been admitted into the ER. Anxiety made my heart pound fast, and although my nausea had disappeared, it was threatening to return, what with Lochlann glaring at me.

"You can't just ignore me," he said.

"Sure I can."

"Then I'll sit here and wait."

He pulled up a chair and sat down, folding his hands, his gaze on me. The direct eye contact made me want to squirm.

I realized in a rush that he had no reason to know about my pregnancy. Had Naoko told him? But she would never. I'd trust Naoko with my life.

"Whoever said I was pregnant?" I said, attempting to sound genuinely confused.

"The nurse did."

I stared at him, shocked and pissed now. "She had no right to tell you that! I'm pretty sure that's a HIPAA violation!"

"A what violation?"

"It's a law about privacy—never mind, it's not important. But she had no right to tell you."

Lochlann finally looked away, his expression now uncomfortable. "She thought we were related."

Now I crossed my arms. "Oh really? And who gave her that idea? Because I'm pretty sure it wasn't *me*."

"Is it so wrong that I was worried about you and wanted to know what was going on? Fine, I lied. I said we were dating."

"That doesn't mean she should've told you!"

Now I realized my words only implicated me further. Great, just great. This was not how I wanted to tell Lochlann I was pregnant. How awkward. And how dare he lie about being my boyfriend just to get information? That was shady. That was low.

Because you haven't lied at all?

"Well, it's not your baby," I said, lifting my chin. "I told you about Steve. He got me pregnant. Not you. So you don't need to be here."

"Maybe not, but where is this Steve? You'd think he'd want to be here."

"He's out of town. He's in Argentina right now and doesn't have a phone."

"Studying...what was it, flamingos?"

"Yes, flamingos. I just found out I was pregnant after Steve left and since he's doesn't get any service, I decided to wait until he returned."

That sounded totally plausible, didn't it? But based on how Lochlann's expression was hardening, he didn't believe me. He just looked *more* pissed, not relieved.

"Stop the lying, Kate," he said, his voice low. "We both know Steve doesn't exist."

"Seriously? I can tell you how I got pregnant, if you want. Steve made one of his best lasagnas ever, and I pretty much tore his clothes off. He's so sexy, you know, just all muscles and arms and legs and—"

Lochlann leaned over, trapping me to the bed—if I wasn't already kind of trapped with this stupid IV thing.

That voice inside my head, the one that warned me not to do stupid things? It was currently screaming at me. But adrenaline combined with fear made me run my mouth off, as my mom had always called it. It was an unstoppable thing when it happened.

"Kate," said Lochlann.

But I didn't hear him, or heed him. "But I haven't told you all about Steve's dick. It's *huge*. It's like a cross between Godzilla and, um, Sasquatch? Well, maybe not. I have no idea what Sasquatch's dick would like. But it's one of those dicks where you're like, shit, it's going to break me in two! It doesn't, by the way. It's awesome. And then we started fucking on the rug because we were too horny to get to the bedroom."

Lochlann was silent for a long moment. To my surprise, his lips curved into what looked like a smile. A grim smile, but a smile nonetheless. "And so you got pregnant after this lasagna-induced fucking?"

"Exactly."

Lochlann still hadn't stood up. In fact, he only leaned closer, and I could feel his warm breath on my face. His dark hair curled against his forehead, and I had to resist the urge to touch it. "If you're going to lie," he said finally, "you should maybe come up with something more plausible."

I scowled. I tried to push him away, but my IV line got mad at me for daring to move. I had to settle for glaring at Lochlann and crossing my arms over my chest.

"Tell me the truth," he said.

What was I so afraid of? God, everything. Saying it out loud made it real. It made us linked for the rest of our lives. This wasn't some "oops sorry" type of thing you could clean up and move on from. This was a *baby*. A real life human being I'd have to care for.

That we'd have to care for.

Tears sprang into my eyes, and I hated myself for my weakness. It was easier for people to think I was just impulsive or wacky. It was worse when anyone saw that I was actually vulnerable.

"Kate," said Lochlann, his tone gentling so much that the tears only increased. "Just tell me: am I the father or no?"

I nodded, my chin trembling. Then I forced myself to say the words: "Yes, you are."

Lochlann's shoulders slumped. He immediately sat back down, putting his face in his hands. Guilt assailed me, even though this wasn't my fault. If anything, it was his fault, since he'd been in charge of the condom.

Lochlann swore something in Irish that I would've demanded to know the meaning of if I wasn't so tired and heartsick.

"I'm sorry for lying," I said into the silence. "I should've told you earlier."

Lochlann blew out a breath. "When did you find out?"

"Two, three weeks ago? I was going to tell you at our last meeting, but you pissed me off so much I thought, screw it. He wouldn't want to know, anyway."

"Why would I not want to know?" Lochlann was incredulous, like I'd told him I was giving birth to an alien. "This is my baby as much as it's yours."

"Yeah, it is, but I don't expect you to *do* anything about it. We'll be fine on our own."

I thought I'd seen Lochlann pissed before, but I hadn't seen Rage Lochlann. Rage Lochlann probably would've Hulked out if he were, you know, Bruce Banner. Instead, he just stood up with murder in his eyes. I'd never thought you could look at a person and think, *huh, he's going to murder me,* but here we were.

"Are you insinuating," he said slowly, deliberately, "that I'd abandon my child? Have nothing to do with him?"

"Or her."

"Boy or girl, it doesn't matter. But I take care of my responsibilities, and even though the timing and circum-stances are less than ideal, I'm not about to let you two rot in the gutter."

"That seems a bit Dickensian, you know."

He didn't seem to enjoy my lighthearted responses. Well, that was how I dealt with tension, so he just needed to chill. "Look, I didn't mean to insult you. I'm just saying I didn't do this on purpose or expect a whole bunch of child support. My family will take care of us, and I'm smart. I'll figure this out."

"Having a child isn't something you just 'figure out.'"

"You make it sound like all parents know exactly what they're doing when they have a kid. Even I know that they don't."

Lochlann looked like he wanted to argue—no surprise there—when a voice from the other side of the partition said, "Mr. Keller, we really do need a urine sample, if you're able."

Apparently Mr. Keller didn't feel like cooperating, because he groused, "I can barely walk. How am I going to piss in a cup without falling on my face?"

"A nurse can assist you with that."

"Only if she's not the last one I had. Looked like my grandma. Don't want my grandma handling my dick, you know."

I had to bite my lip to keep from laughing. Lochlann's hardened expression had melted, and his jaw twitched as he had to keep in his laughter.

A nurse came to help Mr. Keller to the restroom, leaving Lochlann and I with some privacy for a second. Taking my hand, Lochlann squeezed it.

"We'll get through this," he said. "Because we have someone else we have to think of besides ourselves."

I squeezed his hand back. "What about your job? You can't continue to be my advisor. What do I tell people?" That familiar anxiety pooled inside my gut. "If people find out, they'll think I slept with you because I wanted good grades or something. I'm already on thin ice, being one of the few women in the program."

"I have just as many concerns, believe me. My research, my career—all of it is on the line if anyone hears that this is my baby."

"It's not even fair. We had sex before either of us knew who the other was!"

"I doubt the university would care much about the nitty-gritty details."

We both fell silent, especially when Mr. Keller returned to his bed. Apparently he'd "filled the cup up real good."

How nurses kept straight faces around patients like that, I had no idea.

Lochlann was rubbing my palm, the gesture soothing my nerves. I realized right then how much I wanted to lean on him: literally and figuratively. I'd been so scared after finding out I was pregnant, thinking I had to do everything on my own, that having his support meant so much to me. Squishy heart feelings bubbled inside of me—dangerous feelings that could never be acted upon.

"Can I have a hug?" I said quietly.

Lochlann got up to sit on the edge of the bed, and after some maneuvering he wrapped his arms around me. I leaned my head on his chest, the thump of his heart somehow calming. He was so warm and strong. Even if our relationship—whatever it was—was a mess, I knew in my heart of hearts that he'd protect this child no matter what.

He rubbed my back. "How are you feeling now?" he asked quietly.

"Tired. I want to go home."

"I'll stay with you and take you home."

I sighed. "Thank you." Looking into his eyes, I whispered, "I'm sorry, for lying. I don't usually lie, I swear."

Lochlann's hand stilled on my lower back. Before I knew it, he was leaning down and kissing me.

It was a sweet kiss; it was a kiss of mutual comfort. Somehow it was almost more intimate than having sex. It was a kiss that held promises of the future.

When a new nurse came into my room a half hour later to

check my vitals, she asked me my name and birthdate to verify my identity. Lochlann had moved back to his chair, but when he heard my birthdate I saw him still as he did the math.

Oh shit. I'd lied about my age back in Ireland. I'd forgotten about that little white lie. *Shit, shit, shit.* So much for promising that I'd never lie to him again.

"Oh, your blood pressure is a little high. So is your pulse," said the nurse, frowning. "I'm going to check it again in fifteen minutes just in case, okay?

"I think I'm just anxious," I said.

"Well, I think you'll be out of here pretty soon. I'll have the attending come by soon. No reason to be here all night if you don't need to be."

After the nurse left, I beat Lochlann to the punch. "Yes, I lied about my age in Ireland. I'm twenty-two, not twenty-six. I should've told you that as well. At the time, I thought you'd think I was too young." When he didn't reply, I added, "I'm sorry. Again."

He just sighed before shaking his head. "Christ, this is a fucking mess. I've impregnated a twenty-two-year-old girl, who's also my student." He groaned.

"Hey, I could be sixteen and you could be totally screwed. At least I'm an adult. Besides, I'm not a little girl."

He just groaned again. "Please, stop talking."

"I'm trying to make you feel better."

"Well, you're failing miserably."

"Suit yourself."

When Lochlann drove me back to my apartment an hour later, I was tempted to jump out of the car just as it rolled to a stop, mostly so we could avoid any awkward goodbyes. *See you soon, person with whom I am now having a child.*

"I should walk you to your door," he said, surprising me.

My eyes widened. "No, no. It's fine. You're fine. Stay in the car. Besides, there's nowhere to park around here, and you'll block the street since you can park on both sides of the road—"

Lochlann pulled out his phone. "Give me your number. We'll need to coordinate another meeting, but I'd rather not do it over university email."

Ugh, that made it sound so skeevy now. But I gave him my number, because if we were going to make decisions on this little parasite-bean-thing, we'd probably have to do it face-to-face.

I thought of the kiss in the hospital, and my face heated up. It hadn't even been that sexual, yet here I was, getting horny. Clearly, my hormones were making me insane. It didn't help that Lochlann was looking at me with those dark, fathomless eyes of his and making me remember our one night together way back in June.

"Farewell," I blurted, pushing the car door open. "I shall see you soon."

He didn't even smile, the icicle man. "Goodbye, Kate. Take care of yourself until then, otherwise you'll have to answer to me."

CHAPTER TWELVE

KATE

W hat did a girl wear when meeting her baby daddy at his apartment a week after he found out she was pregnant?

A. Sweats and an oversized, stained hoodie, so he couldn't think I wanted him to find me attractive in the slightest

B. Jeans and a t-shirt that had sexy potential but didn't scream BANG ME INTO NEXT TUESDAY

C. A short skirt and tight sweater that basically advertised my legs and how easily they could wrap around his waist

I decided on B after much thought and feedback from Naoko, who eventually told me I wasn't going there for a hookup, anyway.

"You realize if you sleep with him again, you'll be in even more hot water," she said logically.

"I mean, yes, but the cat's already out of the bag on this

one. We might as well enjoy the one benefit we have in this whole thing." I poked at my abdomen. The bump was definitely growing, but it wasn't noticeable unless I was naked. Even then, it looked more like a food baby, not a baby baby.

"Remember, Kate: WWND?"

I rolled my eyes. *What Would Naoko Do*, because Naoko never did stupid things like I did. "You saw him. You'd bang him, too," I said defensively.

"I think your hormones have poisoned your brain. Because there's no way even you would be *that* stupid."

Fine, she had a point. I couldn't really have sex with Lochlann again. It would be the height of stupidity. It would go on record of stupidest thing ever. I'd get a medal that read *Biggest Moron* on it in the mail.

This was what I told myself, even as I waited for Lochlann to open his apartment door. When he did, wearing jeans and a polo shirt, his feet bare, I felt like I was intruding on him. It didn't help that I could see his chest hair, or that he had scruff on his cheeks.

Lochlann looked over my shoulder before ushering me inside. "Did anyone see you?"

I stared at him. "Uh, not that I know of. Why? Are you on some secret spy mission now?"

He gave me an exasperated look. "You and I both know that if you were seen at my flat, this would end badly."

I heard a meow at my feet; a fluffy orange cat weaved around my ankles. I reached down to stroke its head.

"You have a cat?" I said, rather inanely.

"That's Clurichaun."

"What does that mean?"

"It's an Irish sprite that drinks too much."

I laughed. When I bent down, Clurichaun put his paws on my knee, demanding that I continue to pet him.

For some reason, I was surprised that Lochlann had a cat. He seemed like the type of person to have an aversion to animals. Or worse, an entire collection of pet rocks.

"What a lover," I said. "He's adorable."

"He's very flirty with women, I'll say that."

I picked up the cat, enjoying the rumbling of his purr. "My sister Dani has a cat, but he's not as nice as yours. I would've thought you'd have a grumpy, antisocial cat."

Lochlann raised a single dark brow. "Why? Are you saying *I'm* grumpy and antisocial?"

"Noooooooo. Of course not." Except I was smiling as I said the words, and not doing a good job of hiding it.

"You're a pain in my arse, that's for sure." Lochlann motioned to the futon in the living room . "Go sit down. Do you want something to drink?"

"Nope, but thank you." I set Clurichaun down, mostly so I could look around Lochlann's place. There wasn't much to see, honestly: just a futon, a coffee table that had seen better days, and a bookshelf in the corner. A vining plant sat in the window. If Dani were here, she'd be able to identify which plant it was. Me, though? I'd always had a black thumb, despite my family's propensity for gardening.

I'd always done better with the stuff you could light on fire. They were more fun, anyway.

I sat down on the futon, realizing a moment later that this was also Lochlann's bed. A shiver went through me. Naoko's voice inside my head admonished me, though. *WWND? She would not have sex with her graduate advisor on his futon.* Combined with my uh-oh voice, I was thoroughly chastised.

Honestly, if anyone knew how many voices I had in my head I'd probably be committed.

Clurichaun got up and settled on my lap, as if we'd been friends for ages. When Lochlann returned with two bottles of water and a box of crackers, he paused, as if he'd forgotten I were here.

He cleared his throat. "I thought maybe you'd be hungry. I know you said you didn't want anything to drink, but you need to stay hydrated." He handed me one of the bottles of water before sitting down next to me. He put enough space between us that I'd have to reach out to touch his thigh.

So much for coming here to seduce. We were apparently just going to sit in silence as we munched on crackers and stared at the wall. *Awesome.*

It was stupid, but I felt...rejected. Yes, I know, it was stupid. Had I really thought Lochlann would put a hand on my leg, say something sexy, before pushing his futon down to make it into a bed so he could fuck me senseless?

The sad thing was the answer was *almost* yes.

"I apologize for the state of my flat," said Lochlann, breaking the awkward silence. "I haven't had time to furnish it, what with starting this new position and now this." He gestured toward me.

"I mean, you don't have cockroaches running around, so I'd say it's a step up from most college apartments around here."

Lochlann chuckled. "Don't remind me. When I was your age, I lived in a flat with five other guys, and none of us thought it was important to clean. It got to the point that the landlady threatened to evict us because it smelled like something had died."

"You're really giving me some great reasons to trust you with this baby," I joked.

Lochlann's smile faded. "That's something I wanted to discuss with you: your health and that of the baby's. Have you chosen a physician? Do you know where you're going to give birth?"

"Um, in a hospital?" Was there any other place to have a baby?

"More women give birth at home, if the pregnancy is normal and healthy."

I made a face. "Okay, for one, whose home would this birth be taking place? Because I live in a tiny apartment with Naoko, who I doubt would enjoy seeing me push a baby out of my vagina. And your place isn't exactly ideal, either."

"I plan to furnish this place, make it into a real home. But regardless, this is something you need to think about, especially after your visit to the hospital."

I squirmed a little, embarrassed. "I don't go to the ER all that often. Actually, I've only been there once, and that was when I was five and broke my arm after stealing my friend's stuffed animal. I climbed on top of one of those Playhouse things and fell onto the concrete."

"That sounds like something you would do. I'm just surprised it was when you were five, not twenty."

"Okay, rude." I tried to elbow him, but he wasn't quite close enough, so I ended up almost falling onto Clurichaun. Lochlann laughed, helping me sit back up.

"My point still stands," he said. "You need to be watched over. You can't just live with a roommate."

I bristled. "Naoko is my best friend."

"You misunderstand me. She seems like a lovely girl, but what happens if you faint and you're by yourself? What happens when you're near the end of your pregnancy and can't walk up and down stairs like you used to? Things like that."

He had a point. I didn't want things to change, but obviously they were going to. *Time to face the music, Kate.*

"So, am I moving in with you?" I said, jokingly. "Not sure that'd be a great way to keep this a secret."

"Obviously that wouldn't work. No, you'll move into the flat down the hall from me. Its tenant just moved and it's empty at the moment. I took the time to inquire with the landlord and already put a deposit down. You can move in within the next few days."

I stared at him, wondering if he was just messing with me. Had he seriously gotten me an apartment without consulting me? Like I was too stupid to make my own decisions?

"I don't want to move," I said, "and besides, that'd put Naoko in a major bind. She'd have to find a new roommate quickly, and I hate the thought that she'd end up with some creep because I bailed on her."

"Her boyfriend can't move in with her?"

I scowled. "No, he has his own place with roommates and her family would kill her if she lived with him." I waved a hand, annoyed. "That's not the point. The point is that I don't need you taking control of my entire life. Just because you knocked me up doesn't mean you get to tell me what to do."

Lochlann just folded his arms across his chest. "Considering that you got yourself in the ER, I don't think it's out of the bounds of reason to take control of the situation."

I growled, which startled Clurichaun. He jumped down from the futon and gave me a dirty look.

"I am *not* a situation," I said, pointing my finger in Lochlann's face. "I am not your dirty little secret, either. Just because you happen to be older than me does not mean you're smarter, or wiser, or know more shit than me. You know as much about having a baby as I do: aka, none. Unless you have a bunch of other kids you've failed to mention?"

"As far as I'm aware, no, I haven't fathered any more children."

"Oh, well, that's a relief. At least I'll get all of the child support." My voice dripped with sarcasm.

"You're just being stubborn to prove a point. You know as well as I that you moving close to me will be ideal, especially once the baby is here. Are you going raise him or her where you live now? With no help? Have you even told your family that you're pregnant?"

I hated how right he was. I hated that he was tearing my stubborn refusal down, brick by brick. "I haven't figured out how to tell them yet," I hedged.

"So were you ever going to tell anyone? Were you just going to give birth and drop the baby off at the nearest fire station?"

I gasped. "Are you fucking serious right now?"

"Completely serious."

I'd never been the type of person to be violent, but in that moment, I wanted to shake Lochlann. Or punch him in the face.

I might've been thinking of this baby as my little parasite, but the mere thought of abandoning him or her made me want to burst into tears. I touched my abdomen, as if I could shield the fetus inside me from the words being thrown around outside the womb. Protectiveness that I hadn't felt before filled me.

"I might be impulsive and I might be young," I said, my voice just barely steady, "but I'm not heartless. If anyone's heartless, it's you for saying something like that to me." My voice wobbled on the last sentence, and I hated myself for showing weakness in this moment.

When I wiped away a few tears, I heard Lochlann inhale. He cringed. "I'm sorry," he said in a low voice. "That was a shite thing to say."

I sniffled. "It was. You're a dickwad."

He moved toward me and wrapped an arm around my waist. I stiffened, resisting the comfort he was offering, but when he started to rub my back, I melted like a popsicle under the summer sun. I was pretty much putty in this man's hands.

"I know you aren't heartless," he continued, continuing to stroke my back. "I shouldn't have insinuated as much. I'm just worried that because you're so young that you'd get overwhelmed. It's not completely unthinkable, and what with the lying and the secretiveness, it's hard to believe you really want to keep this baby." His hand stilled. "You do want to keep it, right? Christ, I should've asked. I assumed. Stupid of me."

"No, I mean, I do want to keep it." I leaned my head back to look Lochlann in the eye. "I don't know why, exactly. The timing is terrible. I'm too young; we can't even tell anyone about our relationship. I'll have to keep who the father is hidden from my family. It's insane, and yet..." I shrugged and touched my belly. "I'm already attached to the thing. It makes no sense, but that's the truth."

Lochlann covered my hand with his. In that moment, I could almost imagine we could become a family together. That we could raise this baby and be with each other—love each other, even.

It was crazy, ridiculous. Unthinkable. That hope was dangerous, and yet I clung to it anyway.

"How are we going to do this?" I whispered.

Lochlann's hand on my lower back moved upward until he cupped the back of my neck. "I have no fucking idea," he admitted before he leaned down to kiss me.

It felt like coming home. It felt like everything coming together into perfect harmony. Most of all, it felt *good*. I kissed him back, deepening the kiss, and he groaned. His fingers tangled in my hair. Desire immediately roared inside of me.

He'd awakened something inside me that night we'd slept together. Not just for sex—but for this connection. This foundation we'd created together without even knowing it.

"Kate," he said heavily, kissing down my throat. "Why can't I leave you alone?"

"I'm just that irresistible," I joked.

He sucked on my neck, long enough that I knew he'd give me a hickey. I loved it. I wanted to wear his mark, which was totally messed up. As his lips moved downward, leaving wet kisses in their wake, I felt like I was about to come out of my skin.

"I lied that day. When I said I'd forgotten you," said Lochlann. He was pulling at my t-shirt, and soon it was flung away from me. "I haven't stopped thinking about that night, and when I saw you in my office, it was like a dream and a nightmare come true."

"Thank you? I think."

He chuckled before running a hand under my camisole to one of my breasts. "The way you moan my name, how wet you get for me. How tight your pussy was around my cock. I would jerk off thinking about it. Did you know my fingers smelled like your pussy for hours afterward? That I couldn't get the smell of your arousal off of my skin?"

I shivered, and I shivered harder when he lightly pinched one of my sensitive nipples. "I should be grossed out but I'm not. That's fucking hot."

He reached inside my bra, his fingers warm and lightly callused, and when he flicked a nipple with his nail I almost shot out of my skin. Ever since he'd knocked me up, my breasts had gotten extra sensitive, almost to the point of it being painful. Right now, it felt amazing and almost too much. When he began to kiss me and play with my breasts at the same time, I pretty much flooded my panties.

Yeah, I was pretty much a fountain for him. I would've been embarrassed if I weren't so damn horny and desperate.

Lochlann soon took off my camisole and unhooked my bra. He cupped one breast, letting the weight drop into his hand.

"Are they bigger or am I imagining things?" he said,

caressing the underside.

I had to bite my lip to keep from moaning like a crazy person. "Pregnancy apparently does that to you."

He watched my face as he fondled me. "Either you're into this or desperate for me to stop."

"Can I be both?" I hissed when he rolled my nipple between his fingers. "They're just really sensitive."

"Ah." He leaned down and licked one nipple and then the other before blowing on them. The cool air almost made me jump out of my skin.

"Do that again," I said.

He laughed and did as I asked, playing with my breasts until I was about to climb him like the sexy Irish tree that he was. I'd never thought of myself as a sex kitten—I'd been too into science and terrifying boys—but right then I felt like a total seductress. Based on the tent in Lochlann's pants, I was definitely succeeding at this new role.

Lochlann kissed me as he pushed a hand down the back of my jeans. He squeezed my ass. "Are you wet for me already?" he rumbled. He didn't wait for me to reply, but instead trailed a finger down my crack until he reached my sopping wet pussy. I groaned when he rubbed a finger through the folds.

"Damn, you're dripping." He nipped my bottom lip. "Were you wet when I opened the door? Desperate for me to touch you?"

I could barely speak as he played with my pussy. His strokes were light, teasing, edging me but not giving me the satisfaction I sought.

"Tell me, Kate," he growled in my ear. "Tell me how much you want me to fuck you."

His thumb began to rub my clit. "I want you to fuck me so bad," I confessed.

"I thought so. But you're not getting fucked today." He circled my clit again. "But if you want me to make you come, you're going to have to beg."

"You're a dick."

Lochlann pulled his hand from my jeans, his fingers glistening. "If you want me to stop—"

I unzipped my jeans and yanked them and my panties down my legs in record time before clambering into his lap. How had I ended up naked with him fully dressed? Well, it was hot, I had to admit it. Especially when he squeezed my ass again and kissed me deeply.

"You want me to make you come?" He hadn't returned to my pussy, which only ratcheted my desire higher. Damn, he was such a tease and I fucking *loved* it.

"Yes, please." I even batted my lashes for effect.

He smiled, but it was a devious smile. He widened my legs over his lap before playing with me again. The sound of my wet pussy combined with the thrust of his tongue into my mouth made me tremble. I was just on the edge. Pleasure coiled in my belly when he began to rub my clit with the pressure I needed.

"Yes, yes, just like that," I gasped. "Oh God—harder."

"Like this?"

My eyes rolled back inside my head. The combination of his kisses and his agile fingers made me shoot off like a rocket. I came with a loud groan, shaking in his arms. He kissed me and said something in Irish. His touch gentled, but he didn't stop gently petting me as I came down from my orgasm.

"Oh my God," I said finally, still shivering. "I needed that."

He kissed me, but as I climbed off his lap I could feel the air change. His expression closed as I dressed.

Was he regretting this? I felt ashamed suddenly, even though I had no reason to feel that way.

"Kate, you know this was a bad idea," he said finally. "We can't do this again."

I was shaking as I tried to button my jeans, unable to get the stupid button through the hole. "Yeah, I know, I know. I'm your dirty little secret, your baby mama. That's it."

"You're not my dirty little secret. This is just as much about you as it is me."

I finally got my jeans buttoned. "You know what? It doesn't matter. I'm tired. I'm going home." I wanted to go home, eat some Ben and Jerry's, and sulk like the mature adult I was.

Lochlann followed me to his door. "I'll talk to you soon. We need to discuss the apartment."

"Fine." I didn't have the energy to argue at this point.

He kissed my forehead, told me goodbye, and then gently pushed me out his door. I stood outside in the hallway for a long moment.

Had he just *kicked me out?* Impulsively, I gave his door the middle finger, only for Lochlann's neighbor to come out of his apartment at the same time to see me giving an inanimate object the bird.

"You okay, ma'am?" he asked.

"Just peachy. But your neighbor is a dick. In case you didn't know."

"Um, sure thing, ma'am."

CHAPTER THIRTEEN

KATE

My family was a little strange, but we were close. Since my sisters and I all still lived in town, we would go home for dinner a few times a month. The family party had expanded when Dani had started dating Jacob, and then Mari had married Liam. I'd been the one who'd never brought a boy home.

Now two weeks into the quarter, I didn't have a boy to bring home: I had a fetus to bring along with me. And because of that, I'd gotten out of the last two family dinners with excuses that I was too busy studying.

My mom had texted me two days ago, asking me if I'd come to dinner on Sunday. *We haven't seen you in forever!* she lamented, including a long line of sad emoji faces. *And I know you need to use the washer and dryer at some point.*

Okay, she had me there. Although our apartment building had laundry, you had to use coins and it was a huge pain in the ass. My laundry was piling up, and I'd started wearing my underwear inside out to avoid going home to wash them.

So much for proving to Lochlann that I was a mature adult.

Sitting on the couch while Naoko practiced her tuba in her room, I racked my brain for an excuse to get my mom to leave me alone. But it wasn't my mom who got me to go to a family dinner: it was Mari and her guilt trip.

Mom's worried about you, she texted me only a half hour after our mom had messaged me. *She thinks you're upset about something.*

I'm a grad student. We're the flakiest beings on earth.

You live all of two miles away.

I told you guys that I'm busy.

The dreaded blinking dots popped up on my screen, and as they blinked and blinked, I knew Mari was sending me some epic text of doom. I groaned inwardly.

To my surprise, though, the text she finally sent me was short and to the point.

I'd really like you to come to dinner to help me finish preparations on my baby shower. I know you're busy and you weren't asked to coordinate it, but it'd mean a lot to me if you'd still be there.

I groaned aloud. How could I say no to that? The only way I could bail was if I lied about being ill, and if I did that, my sisters and my parents would come to my apartment to check on me.

Okay, I'll be there.

That Sunday, as if overnight, my bump suddenly went from a slight curve to an actual certified bump. To my immense irritation, my jeans were now too tight. I could get them on and buttoned, but the metal button dug into my belly. And, of course, I'd spilled oatmeal all over my one pair of sweatpants: at the moment, they looked like I'd barfed on them.

I realized what I had to do and groaned. I pulled out the one dress I owned—besides the bridesmaid dress I'd bought for Mari's wedding—and put it on. Luckily for me, it was nice and billowy. Add some leggings and a sweater and we were in business.

"So are you going to tell them tonight?" said Naoko as I was about to leave.

I just laughed. I wasn't planning to tell my family until the kid was eighteen. Okay, fine, that was a terrible plan, but I hadn't yet mustered the courage to spill that particular can of beans.

"I'm only going so they don't start sniffing around," I said. "The last thing I need is my parents freaking out."

I wished, suddenly, that Lochlann was going with me. He wasn't even my boyfriend: just my baby daddy. I blushed a little as I thought about how he'd made me come in his apartment, his fingers and his voice joining together to send me over the edge.

He texted me every day, mostly to ask how I was feeling. I almost wished he didn't care because then I could hate him. If I hated him, I could forget about him, at least in terms of being a man I could fall in love with.

That'll never happen. He'll *never let that happen.*

Besides, was I willing to give up all my hard work, my research, my reputation, for a man who might never be anything more than a one-night stand?

When I arrived at my parents' place, it had started raining, and I felt like a cat left out in the rain by the time I got inside.

"Kate, how can you grow up in Seattle and not own a raincoat?" admonished my mom as she bustled me inside. She hugged me, smelling like patchouli, the crystals hanging from her neck gently clinking together. Julie Wright was my opposite in every way: where she believed in the healing power of crystals, I believed in the healing power of antibiotics. Where she believed that tarot could reveal the future, I preferred to leave the whole future thing a secret.

Okay, to be fair, my mom *did* believe in antibiotics. Yet I couldn't tell you how many times I'd get strep throat as a kid and end up with a bunch of blue lace agates on my throat along with the comment from her, *they're clearing your throat chakra, sweetheart.*

"I have an umbrella," I said, wiping the raindrops from my face. "Somewhere."

"Tourists use umbrellas. For shame," said Dani from inside the dining room. I could see her setting plates down on the table with her fiancé, Jacob, helping her.

I have to admit, when I first found out Dani was dating the guy who'd been such a dick to her in high school, I was kinda hoping it was some revenge scheme she'd cooked up. But, no, apparently she and Jacob had actually fallen for each other. Go figure.

I went into the dining room. "Hey, sis, did you ever tell Jacob about the time you went to Pike Place and wet your—"

Dani squawked, interrupting me, at the same time Jacob started laughing.

"Somebody dumped their soda on me! I told you that five thousand times!" Dani scowled at me from the other side of the table.

"Yeah, sure, you just went to the bathroom and came back with your crotch all wet. Sounds logical."

"Katey cat, don't torment your sister. You know she had a small bladder as a child." My mom patted my arm while Dani groaned, Jacob still laughing silently next to her.

I heard my dad's voice from the kitchen. Kenneth Wright was practical where my mom wasn't, but they complemented each other well despite that. They'd managed to start and run my family's flower shop, Buds and Blossoms, successfully.

Although my mom was a total New Age witchy hippie, she had a mind for numbers that lent itself well to keeping the financials of the business in tip-top shape. My dad, though, was the one who'd always been obsessed with plants. His entire office was filled with various orchid species, an affinity I definitely did not share with him.

"Babe, I thought you said you didn't keep any secrets from me," joked Jacob as he followed Dani into the living room.

"It wasn't a secret. It just didn't seem all that important to share," was Dani's wry response.

"Where's Mari and Liam?" I asked my mom as we finished preparing dinner. My dad had been shooed to his office after he'd burned the dinner rolls. Apparently he'd gotten an alert on his phone about a potential new species of orchid that had sent him "into a tizzy," as my mom had put it.

"Mari texted to say they were running late. Apparently they were waiting on some delivery. You kids and your online shopping." My mom clucked her tongue as she tossed the salad. "When I was your age, I loved to go out and shop, but now all of you refuse to leave your house for so much as a tube of toothpaste."

"I mean, why put on pants if you don't have to?"

"I totally agree," rumbled an Irish accent that, for a split second, made me think Lochlann had followed me here. I jumped, the tongs I was holding clattering to the kitchen floor, right as Liam and Mari came in.

"Sorry, did I scare you?" Liam bent down and handed me the tongs. "Didn't think you scared that easy like."

I laughed awkwardly. "No worries. I was listening to Mom complain about you guys waiting for your box of toothpaste."

Mari made a face. "We didn't order a giant box of toothpaste, Mom. It was the crib we ordered. We didn't want the box sitting out in the rain like what happened with the changing table."

"I dunno why we pay for delivery when people here are so bloody shite at it." Liam popped an olive into his mouth.

My mom shot Liam a dark look. "Watch your mouth. You might not be my son by blood, but we don't talk like that in this house."

I couldn't help the laugh that burst forth. "Mom, if I had a dollar for how many times I've heard you say 'fucking hell' when you got a bad tarot reading—"

"You'd be completely broke." My mom turned to get something from the stove, only to almost run into Mari. "Good lord, this kitchen is too small for all of you. Out, out, out!"

As we went down the hallway to the living room to join Dani and Jacob, Mari said to me, "A dress? That's new."

"All of my pants are dirty," I said, which was sort of true but not really.

"Gross, Kate. When's the last time you did laundry? Do I want to know?"

"You probably don't want to know that I'm wearing my underwear inside out, either."

Mari wrinkled her nose, rubbing her baby bump at the same time. "Just don't get too close to me. I'm super sensitive to smells lately."

Seeing my oldest sister sit down next to her husband, his arm slung over her while his other hand touched her pregnant belly, I felt jealousy bubble inside me. Here I was, carrying a secret that felt like it weighed a thousand pounds, and no one in my family seemed to notice. I was just Kate, the sister who was incapable of doing her laundry or coming home when asked.

Kate, the prankster. Kate, the screwup. Kate, the strange nerdy girl who wasn't like anyone else in her family.

Stop feeling sorry for yourself. It's not a good look.

I could tell them, I thought wildly. I could announce it right now, get it off my chest. I could spill the entire story about me, Lochlann, Ireland, sex, fertilization, implantation, all of it. The visit to the ER, Lochlann's plan to have me move in down the hall from him. The way he made me melt with a single touch...

But if Liam found out his cousin had messed around with Mari's younger sister, Liam would kill him with his bare hands. Jacob would probably help, too. The one nice and annoying thing about gaining two brothers-in-law was that they ended up being protective of me along with my two sisters.

"Kate, you okay?" said Dani.

I realized I'd been standing in the doorway, saying nothing, for God knew how long. "I was taking in how disgustingly adorable you all were," I lied, huffing like I was actually annoyed. "It's kind of nauseating, honestly."

"The day you find a guy and fall head over heels for him will be the best day of my life," said Mari.

I grimaced. "That'll never happen." *Because what guy would want to date a woman hung up on her baby daddy?*

"Never say never," said Liam.

Dani turned toward me. "I'm sure there are plenty of single guys in your program. It's like guy city, from what I've heard. You have the pick of anyone you want."

"Wow, how feminist of you," I joked.

Dani shrugged. "I'm not saying you have to marry one of them. Just...have some fun."

I had to bite my tongue in half to keep from laughing and sobbing at the same time. I'd had plenty of fun once— had lost my virginity—and oh, fun fact, I was now pregnant.

"So, in case you were wondering, grad school is going great," I said, changing the subject shamelessly. "So great. Amazing. Let me tell you about all of my classes."

My brothers-in-law and sisters did seem interested in my program, but not for long. I couldn't blame them: most people who weren't in STEM tended to have glazed eyes after five minutes of talking about genomes and biofuels.

"Oh! Did you feel that?" said Mari, grabbing Liam's hand to move it to the other side of her belly. "Wait, maybe it'll happen again."

Everyone fell silent, like their voices could spook Mari

and Liam's baby. Then, a few seconds later, Liam's face split into a wide smile.

"What a kick. She'll be a football player with a kick like that," he said proudly.

Dani came over to feel the baby move, and soon everyone was hovering over Mari, laughing and talking.

I wanted to feel my niece move, I really did, but it was like my limbs were frozen. I couldn't breathe; I couldn't move. The anxiety I'd tamped down for the past two weeks almost choked me right then. When everyone was distracted, I went straight to the bathroom and locked the door.

I sat down on the toilet, my entire body shaking. I didn't cry, though. My abdomen felt tight, and with every gasping breath I made, it tightened further. I lifted up my dress, as if I could see for myself what was wrong. But as far as I could tell, the baby was fine.

I forced myself to take deep breaths, and slowly but surely, my heartbeat calmed and the anxiety seemed to go down. Had that been a panic attack? I'd never had one, but if that was what they were like, it had sucked hardcore.

I didn't know how long I'd been sitting on the toilet before there was a knock on the door. "Kate? Are you almost done? I need to pee and Dad is in the upstairs bathroom right now," said Mari.

Knowing that it'd be pure torture to make a pregnant woman wait to empty her bladder, I opened the door. I forced myself to smile, but based on Mari's confused look, it apparently wasn't convincing.

"Sorry. Go pee before you die," I said hurriedly. I realized I hadn't pulled my t-shirt or hoodie down. Horrified, I yanked them both over my abdomen and practically ran to the dining room.

Throughout dinner, I wondered if Mari had seen that I was pregnant like her. But my bump was just barely a bump, and my dress was billowy enough to cover the lower half, anyway. I kept looking at Mari out of the corner of my eye, but she seemed perfectly unaware of my internal anguish.

I tried my best to interject a joke or a sarcastic aside as the conversation allowed. I told my family about school—giving my best bland expression as I mentioned my advisor offhandedly.

"It's super random that your advisor, of all people, would be Liam's cousin," said Dani. "I mean, it's a specialized field, but he can't be the only professor they considered hiring."

"It happened for a reason. The universe brought him into your life because he had something that only he could provide you," said my mom.

I almost choked on my bite of salad when she said that. *She has no idea exactly what he has "provided" already.*

After dinner, the family ended up back in the living room to chat and play some card games. I considered making an excuse that I needed to go home when Mari cornered me in the kitchen.

"What is going on with you?" she said, her hands on her hips. "You've been acting weird all night."

I stuffed a cookie into my mouth. "Haf not," I said, my mouth full.

Mari held up her hand. "You're wearing a dress," she said, ticking off her fingers. "You barely talked at dinner. You only made *one* joke about Dani buying a plant called

124

Hooker's Lips. And you acted like your research is boring to you, which is completely abnormal. Either you're planning some epic prank or something is up."

I hated how easily my oldest sister could see through me. Dani was easier to manage. Maybe it was because Mari had taken on a motherly role in regards to me since she was nine years older. Not that our own mom hadn't been motherly, but it was just one of those things eldest sisters did.

Right in that moment, I desperately wanted to confide in someone. Considering Mari had done a crazy thing two years ago, marrying Liam in a drunken Vegas ceremony, she'd probably be understanding.

"You can't tell anyone else," I said. I looked around us, especially as the voices in the living room got louder. Grabbing Mari's hand, I hauled ass to my old bedroom upstairs and locked the door.

"What in the world? Who did you kill, Kate? Are you going to jail?"

"I wish."

Mari just crossed her arms, her foot tapping against the floor.

I sighed and collapsed onto my twin bed. My room was almost exactly as I'd left it: the walls covered in Bill Nye motivational posters, the bookshelf mostly filled with books about genetics, along with a smattering of romance novels. The romance novels were one of my guilty pleasures—even nerdy science girls needed to read some sexy cunnilingus scenes, okay?

When I sat down on the bed, though, my dress settled over my bump like a flashing-red sign. I didn't have time to mess with it before Mari pounced on me.

"Katherine Lydia Wright, I sincerely hope that's a food baby from gaining the freshman fifteen."

I burst into tears. Ugly, noisy, pathetic tears. Mari sighed and, sitting next to me, pulled me into a tight hug. She murmured things into my hair, and finally, after some time, I calmed down enough to give her the details of everything that had happened in the past three months. Although Mari's eyes widened as I gave her the details, she let me speak without interruption, for which I was thankful. I didn't have the strength to deal with recriminations right then.

"Oh, Kate," she said softly. She tucked a strand of hair behind my ear. "This is quite a scrape, even for you."

I sniffled. "Tell me about it."

"You can't hide this forever. What are Mom and Dad going to think when you come home one day with a baby?"

"I know, I know. I know what I'm doing isn't logical or responsible, at least in terms of hiding the pregnancy. But if the truth comes out, Lochlann could lose his job, and I could lose my place in the program. At the very least, my reputation would turn to shit. Nobody would take me seriously after this."

Mari's expression hardened. "You know I have to tell Liam about this."

At that, I grabbed my sister's hands. "You can't. Liam will spill the beans and murder the father of my baby. Do you want your husband in jail? Because you know he'd lose his damn mind."

Mari considered my plea before finally sighing. "Fine, fine. You're right. He would not handle it well." She pointed a finger at me. "But that doesn't mean Lochlann gets off the hook. I could strangle him myself! Getting my little sister pregnant? Sleeping with a girl who's, what? Fifteen years his junior?"

"He's only ten years older than me, and I might've fudged my age when we met."

Mari sighed again. "Of course you did. Did you ever once think about what you were doing? That having unprotected sex could lead to pregnancy?"

"We used a condom!" My voice was so loud that Mari shushed me. "We used a condom," I repeated in a lower voice. "We weren't total idiots. It just didn't fucking work."

"So what *are* you going to do? Do you have any plans beyond keeping this a secret forever?"

I realized that I had to make a decision. If I wanted this baby to have a good life, I couldn't sit around feeling sorry for myself. Although I hated how he'd made the decision without asking me, I knew Lochlann was right about me moving into his apartment complex. It would be the next best thing to actually living together.

As far as keeping this baby a secret? I couldn't do that. Not any longer.

But I'd have to keep the father's identity a secret. At least until...I didn't know. For as long as necessary.

As Mari and I made our way back downstairs, I said sort of jokingly, "So on a scale of one to ten, how freaked out do you think Mom and Dad will be when I tell them I'm having a bastard child and I won't tell them who the father is?"

Mari, bless her, just gave me a not-so reassuring pat on the arm.

CHAPTER FOURTEEN

LOCHLANN

Kate looked me up and down, a comical expression on her face. "Are you seriously in disguise?"

"I'm making it harder for people to recognize me, yes."

"You really should've bought a fake beard. Maybe a fedora, too. Then again, no one would believe you managed to knock up a woman wearing either of those."

I scowled down at her. She giggled, which charmed me despite the insane circumstances we found ourselves in. Today was Kate's eighteen-week ultrasound, and the first one I'd been able to attend. I'd tried to attend earlier ones, but finding someone to substitute for my classes without someone getting suspicious would've been impossible.

"Come on, James Bond. We're gonna be late," said Kate.

When we sat down in the waiting room, I sat three seats down from Kate so if someone who knew us happened to stroll by, they wouldn't see anything untoward.

Just a male professor waiting to see an OB-GYN. *What would be strange about that?* I thought wryly.

The weekend prior, Kate had moved into the flat down the hall from me. I'd been stupid enough to think that helping her move in wouldn't be something anyone would notice. But of course, one of the movers was a student from my freshman materials class. The section included over one hundred students, so although the student had recognized me, I hadn't recognized him.

"Dr. Gallagher? What're you doing here?" He'd given me a look up and down, then glanced at Kate. "You two know each other or something?"

Kate and I both replied at the same time, "No!"

Considering I was standing in Kate's kitchen, holding a box that held her pots and pans, this particular student gave us both a strange look. "Um, okay. Let me get Jack so we can get the couch in here."

That incident had only hit home how precarious this situation was. If one person suspected, if one person saw us together and thought we were romantically involved, it'd be all over. I'd be sent straight back to Dublin, all of my hard work thrown in the rubbish bin. And what would happen to Kate and the baby? I couldn't continue to live in the country if my work visa were revoked as a result of losing my position.

Of course, Kate and I could marry. I'd do it, even though I knew I wouldn't be the type of husband she needed or deserved. But how could I ask her for that sacrifice? To marry a man who'd always love his research more than his wife?

We were between a rock and a hard place, because I'd been fucking stupid enough to give in to a night of indulgence. For two years, I'd managed to avoid any entanglements with women. Apparently my self-control was not as strong as I'd thought—when I'd seen Kate, I'd known she was mine.

She's not anything but the mother of your child, I reminded myself as I followed Kate after her name had been called. I resisted the temptation to hunch into the collar of my jacket, as if I were ashamed of being here.

After the nurse instructed Kate to get on the exam table, I instinctively took her arm to help her up there. Kate, though, jerked in surprise, her eyes widening.

"Um," she said. She shoved her arm at me. "Sorry. I mean, I'm fine. I'm not that fat yet."

I cleared my throat and nodded. The nurse looked perplexed by our interaction, but she was too much of a professional to comment. After she'd taken Kate's vitals, Kate and I waited for her doctor.

Kate's legs swung, her heels lightly bouncing against the metal table. I couldn't help but marvel at how her belly had grown in the past few weeks. Her pregnancy was now more apparent, but a combination of loose pants and sweatshirts had enabled her to keep it hidden from the general public.

"Kate, hello," said Dr. Sanders. "And you must be the father. Nice to meet you."

"Lochlann," I said as I shook her hand. Dr. Sanders was a short, compact woman, her face deceptively young. In contrast, her hair was snow white. She could've been any age between twenty-five and fifty-five.

"How are you feeling? No more dizziness, nausea?" Dr. Sanders washed her hands before instructing Kate to lie down.

"Nope. I've been feeling way better than in the first trimester," said Kate.

"Excellent. That's pretty common. The second trimester is when you aren't so big that you're uncomfortable, but your morning sickness and other symptoms often disappear. I'm going to measure you and then we'll get to the ultrasound."

Dr. Sanders measured Kate's belly, which I'd learned was one of the ways they checked to see if the baby was growing as it should. Every time I waited for Dr. Sanders to pronounce something healthy, I held my breath. After that visit to the ER, I'd had to restrain myself from being over-protective, watching over Kate as best I could, given that we couldn't let anyone know we were, in fact, having a child together.

Part of me almost wanted to reveal everything. Keeping this a secret was draining: not just for me, but for Kate, too. The dark circles under her eyes weren't simply because she was both a student and a woman growing a baby inside her. I knew the effort of keeping my paternity a secret weighed on her, and I bloody fucking *hated* it. I blamed myself. I should've made certain the condom wasn't defective.

I should've never fucking touched her.

"Everything looks and sounds normal. Okay, lift your shirt and pull down your pants some. That's good, perfect," said Dr. Sanders. "Now, sorry about the cold goo. I promise it's supposed to be cold for a reason."

Kate winced when the cold goo hit her abdomen, but when Dr. Sanders began to use the wand to search for the baby, I found myself completely mesmerized.

"You'll have a better view here," said Dr. Sanders, pointing to the chair next to Kate's head.

I hadn't moved from the chair in the corner. When Kate gave me a small nod, I went to sit next to her, my heart hammering.

"Oh, there's baby." Dr. Sanders pointed to the screen. "There's an arm. See that? Looks like baby is waving."

I couldn't help it: I grabbed Kate's hand. I felt as though the breath had left my body. There was our baby, protected inside Kate's womb, growing as it should. This little baby was something we'd created together. As Dr. Sanders moved the wand around Kate's belly, pointing out various body parts, I was overwhelmed.

Joy, terror, pride—too many emotions to name. As I looked at my baby—*our* baby—it was as if everything coalesced into this perfect, crystal clear moment. Everything became real.

This was happening. Kate and I were having a baby.

In that moment, the regret, the fear, the guilt—it melted away like snow in the sunshine. This baby was something I would never regret. As I watched Kate's face split into a wide smile, I knew I'd never regret meeting her and having this baby with her, either.

"Did you two want to find out the gender today?" Dr. Sanders moved the wand again. "If baby will just turn our way, that is. He or she has decided they'd rather show us their backside."

Kate laughed. "That sounds like my kid." She turned to me. "I wanted to find out the gender because there's no way I'd have the patience to wait. How about you?"

"Don't most people find that out these days?"

"Yeah, but some people like it to be a surprise," said Kate.

"Considering everything, I'm not sure either of us need another surprise."

Kate wrinkled her nose. "What? Like the baby is actually going to be a shark or something? I'm pretty sure we only have two choices here."

I squeezed her hand. "You're a pain in my arse, you know that?"

"So that's a yes?"

"Yes, that's a yes."

Dr. Sanders chuckled. "Well, perfect timing, because this baby has just given us a nice view. It's a girl. See the vulva here?"

Kate leaned forward. "I see it! Oh my God, our child has no shame. I love it." Her eyes lit up as she stared at the screen. "A girl." When she turned back towards me, she had tears in her eyes. "A little girl, Lochlann."

A little girl. I'd never thought I'd have children—not after Sophie had left me. The thought of caring for, protecting, and loving a daughter overwhelmed me. Would she be impulsive and fiery like her mother? Or would she be more introspective and deliberate like me?

I couldn't help myself. I kissed Kate, right then and there in the doctor's office. Kate made a surprised sound in the back of her throat, but she kissed me back. It was only the sound of Dr. Sanders moving the ultrasound cart that made us jump apart.

When we arrived back at my flat, I said quietly to Kate, "Can you come in for a moment?"

After I'd closed my door, my body hardened at the realization that we were alone for the first time in weeks. I hadn't let myself be alone with her for this very reason. Seeing her now, her belly rounded with our daughter, her cheeks slightly flushed, I knew that if I kissed her again we wouldn't stop until we were on the floor, fucking each other senseless.

I swallowed. I couldn't let that happen. I'd already gone too far when I'd given in to temptation and made her come on the futon only a few feet away from us.

"I just wanted to say that, no matter what happens, I'll take care of you and our daughter," I said in a rush.

"I never doubted you would."

To my surprise, she wrapped her arms around me, and I allowed myself to hug her back. Resting my chin on top of her head, I murmured, "I don't want you to feel like you're alone in this. Because you're not."

"I might not have believed you saying that before, but I do now." Kate looked up at me. "I know neither of us had this in our plans, but if I had to have a bastard child with anyone, I'm glad it's with you."

I clucked my tongue. "Our daughter is not going to be called a bastard child, because this isn't the nineteenth century."

"Thank God. Otherwise I would've had to marry you."

I stilled; Kate blushed when she saw my expression and immediately broke our embrace.

It was stupid, the hurt that made my heart tear inside me. The last thing either of us needed was to get ourselves trapped in an unwanted marriage.

So why did I feel like she'd just punched me in the gut? It made no sense. Because if I were developing feelings for this brilliant, frustrating, gorgeous woman...it'd be catastrophic.

Kate fiddled with her hair. "I should go. Thanks for coming with me today. Doing all of this alone..." She wrung her hands. "It's been scary. And overwhelming. So I'm glad you're around, I guess."

I took her hands, squeezing them. "I'm going to keep staying around. I can promise you that."

Kate's genuine thank you sent an arrow straight through my heart. I let her go, although part of me wanted her to stay. I wanted to talk about the future. I wanted to talk about baby names, and how to decorate the nursery. I wanted to talk about the things you talked about with the mother of your child.

The weight of the world suddenly pressed down on my shoulders. I'd never felt torn in so many directions at once: protectiveness over Kate, happiness for our daughter, and absolute terror that all of this would coming crashing down like a house of cards at any moment.

In that moment, I rather desperately wanted to tell my parents everything. As a boy, my mam had always been the one to fix things, while my da would never fail to give me advice when I couldn't figure out a problem.

But I wasn't a child anymore. I couldn't run to my mam, crying, and have her bandage my knee. And if I told them I was having a baby, they would lose their minds and would understandably want to know all the details.

As if the universe wanted to make me feel even guiltier, a text message from my mam flashed on my phone. *Wanted to let you know that we're proud of you! Love you.*

My thumb hovered over the call back button. The

impulse was so strong that I didn't know how I managed to overcome it.

I couldn't burden my parents with this, and I sure as hell couldn't lose my job—the job they'd done so much to help me get in the first place. And the job that would help care for them as they got older.

No, this was my burden. I might not know what I was going to do from day to day, but I was determined to do the best I could. Kate and our daughter deserved that much.

CHAPTER FIFTEEN

KATE

As the quarter continued on, I found myself becoming immersed in schoolwork. It was a welcome distraction, what with the whole "living down the hallway from my baby daddy" thing. Every day when I came home from class, I passed by Lochlann's apartment. More than once, I'd stood outside his door, my fist lifted to knock, only for me to chicken out and scamper home.

Lochlann had been distant lately. He'd been attentive as much as he could be, but whenever I'd try to talk about anything other than the baby or mundane things like the weather, he'd immediately change the subject. Anything that alluded to me and him becoming an *us* was especially touchy.

I knew we couldn't be a couple. I knew that, and yet what I wanted refused to match up with what I knew was logical. I'd always prided myself on my ability to be practical, logical. Scientific. The data told me the fallout from being open about our relationship would be worse than being together would be good.

I knew that. I'd even written down the pros and cons so I could see it in print.

But sometimes the heart wanted what the heart wanted. And my heart was fucking stupid.

On a rainy day a week before Halloween, I was spending my evening writing a report for my optoelectronics course that I'd been procrastinating. I enjoyed research, but the reports made me want to light myself on fire. Maybe someday I'd be so powerful that I'd never have to write reports again.

More and more, I'd been feeling the baby move. I'd often wake up in the morning, feeling this little girl kick me in my kidneys or press on my bladder, and I'd coo like it was the most adorable thing ever. Which it was.

I'd fallen in love with this parasite-baby, the booger. I'd tried to keep myself detached. I'd tried to act like it was no big deal, because, Denial with a capital D.

When my phone chimed with a message, I instantly hoped it was Lochlann, only to see it was my mom. *I'd really like to discuss you moving home,* she wrote. *I don't see how you're going to take care of a baby by yourself. You have no idea what it's like to care for a newborn!*

My parents were trying their hardest to twist my arm to move back home. I'd been tempted, I had to admit. But if I did that, there was no way Lochlann could be the father he wanted to be. The second he showed up at my parents' place, admitting he was the father, my parents would kill him—if Liam didn't do it first.

I ignored my mom's message, only for her to send another flurry of messages.

I also don't understand why you moved into another apartment instead of moving home.

And why are you keeping the father secret? I have to admit, I'm hurt that you feel like you can't trust me, and it worries me.

Should we be worried for your safety?

Kate, please answer.

I sighed, sending a message assuring my mom for the millionth time that I was safe, that I appreciated her concern, but that I was an adult and didn't need her to question my choices, strange as they seemed.

"Of course you'd create all of this drama before you were born," I said to my belly, poking at it lightly. "I'm kind of terrified what you're going to be like, honestly. But in a good way."

The baby moved and then kicked me. I laughed, wondering if she was protesting that she was already a drama queen.

Right then, there was a knock on my door. Lochlann came inside—I'd given him my spare key, which he'd taken reluctantly before I'd convinced him it was simply out of practicality.

"Oh, come over here," I said, standing up. When he reached me, I grabbed his hand and placed it on my belly. Our baby had stopped kicking already.

"Was she kicking?" he asked.

"Yes, but now she's stopped, the brat. No, wait, keep your hand there. She'll probably do it again."

We waited in silence, like we'd spook her if we kept talking. Then, another kick. I moved Lochlann's hand a few inches to the left.

"Feel that? Geez, she's really going at it tonight."

Lochlann didn't say anything for a long moment. He was staring at my belly, awe on his face. He'd yet to feel our baby move, mostly due to our not living together. More often than not, this kid liked to move when I was peeing, taking a shower, or trying to fall asleep.

"That's amazing," he said. He moved his hand around my belly. "Does she do that often?"

"More and more, yeah. She's busy tonight. Probably because I had some spicy curry."

Lochlann frowned. "Is that a good idea?"

I almost laughed, but I bit the inside of my cheek instead. "It's fine. The only side effect would be some killer heartburn for me. Or maybe gas. That happens a lot, too."

"I'm so glad you feel comfortable enough to tell me about your propensity for flatulence."

"Hey, man, pregnancy is hella sexy. Gas and heartburn like nothing else. Apparently I can look forward to hemorrhoids and peeing a little when I sneeze in the third trimester, too."

His lips twitched. Was I embarrassed, talking about bodily functions with the man I wanted to bone? Not really. Not if it could make him smile.

God, I was so gone for him. If anything was embarrassing, it was that.

He glanced over my shoulder at my open laptop. "Working on that report? Isn't that due tomorrow?"

I put my hands on my hips. "Your point? I'm doing it. It will be turned in on the deadline. And you're not even the professor for that class, so how did you know about it?"

"You've mentioned it a time or two lately. You've also had over two weeks to finish it."

"If you came over here to procrastination shame, then you can leave." I made a shooing motion. "Besides, in my apartment, you aren't my advisor. You're my baby daddy."

At that, his expression turned cold again, like I'd thrown a bucket of ice water on him. *Good job, Kate.*

"Thank you for the reminder," was his chilly reply. "I only wanted to check when your next ultrasound appointment was."

I could've smacked myself. Gritting my teeth so I didn't say anything worse, I said calmly, "I wanted to make sure you could come, so I haven't made it yet."

"I appreciate that. I'll text you my schedule for the next two weeks."

I felt like we were in his office, and he was acting like my advisor. The distance between us seemed to stretch until I wasn't certain we could ever cross it.

But wasn't this what we both wanted? To keep each other at arm's length?

Fuck that. I'm tired of holding myself back. I'm getting what I want: and that's Lochlann Gallagher.

As seductively as I could, I unzipped my hoodie and tossed it to the ground. Walking toward Lochlann, I then stripped out of my camisole, now wearing nothing but a bra and sweatpants.

Lochlann's eyes darkened. "What the bloody hell are you doing?"

"What does it look like I'm doing? I'm seducing you."

He barked out a laugh, but the laugh dried up in his throat when I unhooked my bra, letting it fall down my arms and to the floor. Pregnancy had made my breasts bigger, my nipples darker, too. At first I'd found it strange, even unsexy, how my body was expanding and shifting to sustain the life inside me.

But the look on Lochlann's face made me realize he didn't have a single complaint about my changed body.

"What are you doing to me?" His voice was a growl.

"Didn't I already explain what I was doing? Or do you want me to spell it out for you?"

Lochlann stared at my breasts, but he hadn't touched me yet. I could feel the desire pulse between us, like a wave of heat. My pussy grew wet simply from the way he looked at me.

"You're so sure of yourself, aren't you? That you can talk to me like that and get away with it." He pushed my sweatpants down my ass to reveal my panties. "But that's where you're wrong, Kate: I call the shots here."

"You say that, and yet I'm not convinced."

The only warning I had was his devious smile before he lifted me into his arms and carried me to my bedroom. I yelped in surprise.

"If you weren't pregnant," he said, "I would've thrown you over my shoulder."

"Um, thanks?"

He set me down on the bed before yanking my sweatpants and panties off. "Look at you: your tits are magnificent."

I pushed my breasts together. "They're kinda big, honestly. I've never realized how annoying boob sweat is until now."

"Your seduction skills need work."

Yet he still took one of my nipples into his mouth, rolling it around with his tongue. Soon he was sucking on one nipple and then the other, the pressure just barely enough. I scraped my nails through his scalp.

I'd instinctively parted my legs, and he'd settled between them. I felt his erection press against my pussy. I lifted my hips, needing more of that hardness against my clit. I moaned when he rolled away from me.

"Lean over the desk," he instructed.

"What happens if I don't?"

He tangled his fingers in my hair, pulling hard enough to make my head tip back.

"You get punished. Like that," he said.

I stuck out my lower lip, but I would be a liar if I said I wasn't enjoying his show of dominance. I wanted him to keep doing it.

He let go of my hair, only to begin to unfasten his pants. I watched as he undressed, my mouth watering as he revealed his body. By the time he revealed his cock I was practically drooling. I got up from my knees to wrap my fingers around it, but after only a few strokes he pushed my hands away.

"What did I say? Lean over the desk."

This time, I did as he demanded. But apparently I was too slow to comply, because Lochlann spanked me once, twice, three times—hard enough to sting, and hard enough to make my pussy pulse with want.

And then, before I realized what was happening, he was behind me on the floor, pushing my legs apart. I felt his tongue on my pussy and almost exploded right then and there.

He chuckled. "So wet already. Did you like getting

spanked?" Rubbing my ass cheek, he then smacked it hard. "You're dripping for me."

I blushed to the roots of my hair, embarrassed and aroused at the same time. He'd never gone down on me, and having his face so close to my pussy was almost unbearably intimate.

"Lochlann..."

"I know. I'll take care of you."

And he did. He licked me from clit to taint, even rubbing my asshole and making me squeak in surprise. He laughed again. If I weren't so aroused, I would've kicked him for laughing at me.

"You're adorable." Lochlann pushed a finger inside my dripping pussy at the same time he kissed my clit. "I want to make you come with my mouth."

I didn't have any quick-witted response to that. I felt an orgasm building inside me already. When Lochlann began fucking me with his fingers and licking at my clit at the same time, I had to bury my face in my arm to keep from screaming like a banshee.

"I'm coming," I gasped. "Oh my God!"

Lochlann groaned, lapping at my pussy as I shook with my release. I'd barely registered that he'd stood up before I felt the tip of his cock at my entrance. He pushed inside in one long stroke, both of us groaning loudly as he filled me.

"Fuck, you're so tight." He pulled out and slammed back into me. "Your pussy is gripping my cock like a vise."

I couldn't breathe. I could only feel Lochlann's cock inside me, pounding into me. He grunted. I felt his balls slap against my clit, and the stimulation was enough for another orgasm to begin coalescing inside me.

He reached down to fondle my breasts, his thrusts getting faster. I felt his cock swell at the same moment he swore something in Irish.

"I'm filling you up, baby. Can you feel it?" He squeezed my breasts. "I'm filling this pussy up until it can't take any more of my cum."

His dirty talk sparked something inside me, wild and insatiable. I came hard a second time, screaming and not caring if anyone heard me.

When we finally collapsed onto the bed together, he curled behind me, placing a protective palm on the mound of my belly. Our daughter had decided to take a nap during that sex session—probably for the best, honestly.

Lochlann kissed my neck, my cheek. His voice rumbled in my ear as he said, "I didn't kiss you. I was too distracted."

I giggled and turned over. "Then how about we make out right now to make up for it?"

Luckily for us both, Lochlann had no more protests to give.

CHAPTER SIXTEEN

KATE

I woke up to the smell of coffee. Groaning, my bladder protesting, I wondered who could be making coffee when I remembered: Lochlann. Last night. Sex.

Oh. My. God.

I blushed like an idiot as the memories flooded back. I'd thrown myself at him like some shameless hussy and he'd called my bluff. We'd had sex twice more during the night, completely insatiable for each other.

I glanced at my phone; it was still early in the morning. Thankfully, my report that I'd neglected last night wasn't due until later that afternoon.

After I peed, brushed my teeth, and attempted to get the knots out of my hair, Lochlann was already sitting in my living room.

"I made you some coffee," he said, as if I hadn't already smelled it from my bedroom.

I sat down next to him and sighed happily. "My one indulgence I'm allowed to have."

Lochlann watched me as I sipped my coffee, as if he'd never seen someone like me before. I had to restrain myself from hiding behind my hair.

Finally, he cleared his throat. "We should talk about last night."

My brain thought: *do we have to?*

My mouth said: absolutely nothing.

"I know I kept saying that this could never happen again," he said, tapping his long fingers against his knee. "But clearly we can't stay away from each other."

I just sipped my coffee and waited.

"But given our close quarters, the likelihood that we'll avoid temptation after last night is pretty much nil. So I propose that we shift our arrangement somewhat: sex as needed, but still keeping it secret."

My fingers gripped the handle of my mug until my knuckles turned white. "So, friends with benefits on the down-low?"

"Essentially, yes."

I felt strangely hurt, although at least he wasn't trying to be so stubborn to deny how explosive the sex had been last night. Had I really expected him to declare his love for me this morning? Cook me some waffles and spell I LOVE YOU in maple syrup on them?

"Do you really think that's a good idea?" I said.

He shot me a wry look. "No. It's a terrible idea. I'm just trying to be practical here. The only other solution is for me to move to another flat, but that leaves you in the lurch. I'm not about to let you live on your own with our baby about to be born."

"We're still six months out, though."

"That's not that much time. It'll go by faster than you think."

I sighed, feeling a headache start to form. "Look, I don't disagree with you. We have a ton at stake here if someone finds out and decides to snitch on us. But I'm tired of fighting what's between us. Aren't you?"

When he didn't answer for a long moment, my heart started pounding with fear. Finally, he smiled, albeit a little sadly.

"When it comes to you, Kate Wright, I'm completely hopeless for you."

I set my coffee down before snuggling up against him. He was basically like a walking, breathing space heater. He put his arm around me. In that moment, we didn't need to speak. I also felt safer than I had in a long time.

Lochlann stroked my hair with gentle fingers. "I'm sorry I can't offer you more than this," he said quietly.

"More than what?"

"Just sex. Comfort. You deserve more than that, but I'm not the man who can give them to you."

I wasn't sure what to say to that. My heart leapt into my throat as I waited for him to explain.

"I was actually in a long-term relationship. We were engaged, too. Her name was Sophie. I thought she was the person I was going to spend the rest of my life with."

"But...?"

He sighed. "But, I was too obsessed with my work. I eventually took our relationship for granted. Sophie pretty much got fed up and ended things, telling me that she wasn't going be second place to my research."

"I'm sorry, but I guess I don't see how that means you can't have *any* relationship? You and Sophie didn't work out. Lots of couples don't work out."

"You don't understand." Lochlann bent his head, sighing. "I loved Sophie. She was the love of my life the day I met her, but she would always be second place to my work. While we were together, I thought she was okay with that. She waited for me to finish my PhD before we got engaged."

My eyes widened. "How many years were you together?"

"Seven before we were engaged, then two after that."

"Damn. You waited seven years to propose? Poor Sophie. I'd be pissed too."

I said the words jokingly, but Lochlann didn't seem to find them funny.

"That's what I mean," he said in frustration. "I don't have the capacity to give what a real relationship needs. I'll always be too immersed in my work that it'll be set off to the side."

"You can't do both? Lots of people do both."

"I tried that, and I failed. Miserably." He shook his head. "And the thing is, Sophie wasn't wrong. I'd neglected her and our relationship. I took her for granted, and I don't want to do the same thing to any other woman." His gaze met mine. "To *you*. We've already got to a point where we have a somewhat amicable relationship. Why ruin it by trying something I already know won't work?"

I had to restrain myself from growling like a crazy woman. "I'm pretty sure one failed attempt does not mean you can't do better next time."

Lochlann's smile was sad. "That's the thing: I don't want

to do better. My research will always come first. I accept that, and I'd imagine you've had similar concerns. Why else did you stay a virgin until you were twenty-two? You said men found you intimidating. That sounds like they knew you couldn't give them your entire heart, because such a huge part of it was already wrapped up in your work."

I wanted to deny it; I wanted to tell him I'd never had that worry. But I'd be lying. Meeting Lochlann had made me think I'd found a man who could keep up with me.

Apparently I'd been wrong about that, too.

"Then I'm sorry," was all I could manage to eke out.

Lochlann stroked my cheek before returning to stroke my hair. "Don't be. It was my own fault. But I owe Sophie a debt. She showed me that I don't have the capacity to have a wife and my career. It was always going to be one or the other."

Lifting my chin, Lochlann explained, "That's why I can't give you anything more than sex. I'll be a father to our daughter, of course. But I'm not the type of man who can put effort into a relationship like it needs without sacrificing my ambitions. Do you understand?"

I did, and yet I didn't. "Are you saying you can't love anyone?"

"This isn't about love. Not really. It's about under-standing my own limitations."

He sounded so sure, like he had already run the data and knew what the outcome was. My stomach twisted. Had I really thought our relationship could become something more? Something beyond sex and mistakes?

"I appreciate you being honest. I wish I could judge you,

but I can't. I've always wondered the same thing about myself," I said. "Could I really have a career and a family? Or would my husband eventually resent me? So I almost got to the point where I told myself I'd rather be alone and have a career than give up such an important part of myself."

"Never give up that part of yourself. Do you hear me?"

I looked up, Lochlann's serious tone surprising me.

"You're absolutely bloody brilliant, Kate. One of the smartest students I've met in a long time. You have a huge career in front of you. I know it. And I'm going to do everything in my power to help you achieve your goals, even with this pregnancy making things complicated."

My heart swelled like the Grinch, growing three sizes too big. I didn't understand why a man who could say such things would believe he couldn't have a career and a family. But if he'd already come to that decision, I knew I didn't have the power to sway him—not when he didn't, and couldn't, love me.

"What if I can't do it?" I whispered.

Lochlann frowned. "I don't understand. Can't do what?"

"Have a career and be a mom. Men can have both, but it's like when you become a mother, that becomes your only identity." I rubbed my belly, tears forming in the corners of my eyes. "I love this baby more than I can say, but I don't want to lose *me*. Is that stupid? Am I just being selfish?"

"Come here." Lochlann folded me into a hug. "That's not selfish. That's a valid fear, but you're forgetting one crucial data point here."

I sniffled. "What?"

"You. Do you think you'll let that happen? You're the most stubborn woman I've ever met, and I'm fucking Irish."

That made me laugh even as a few tears rolled down my face.

"You'll earn your degree. You'll continue your research. And you'll be an amazing mother. Don't doubt that."

Even as I basked in the glow of his words, I didn't understand why he refused to think of himself in such a way. He refused to let me limit myself, yet he was so sure limiting himself was the only possible choice. It didn't make any sense.

I couldn't help but ask, "Why can I have it all, but you can't?"

"Some people just aren't meant to have everything they want," was his cryptic reply.

"That sounds like you're deflecting."

His lips twitched. "And you're a pain in the arse." Rubbing my back, he added, "Don't you have a report to finish?"

"Don't remind me. I'm so tired; my brain is total mush."

Lochlann's smile transformed his face, and my stupid heart skipped a beat. "Are you saying I kept you up past your bedtime?"

"Way past my bedtime. I barely got any sleep thanks to you."

"I'd apologize, except I'm not sorry."

"Neither am I."

He kissed me, his lips molding to mine like they were meant for me. His scruff scratched my chin. I licked at his lips, and soon we were making out when we definitely had more pressing concerns. He had to get to class, and I had to finish this report.

But I indulged myself for a bit longer, because I didn't know when I'd get another chance. Just because Lochlann said he wanted to keep sleeping with me didn't mean he wouldn't freak and run the opposite way when he thought about it harder.

"What do you think she'll be like?" I said after our kissing had devolved into cuddling again.

He didn't need me to explain who "she" was. "She's going to be absolutely terrifying."

"Well, that's rude. What a thing to say about your daughter." I tried to sound offended, except I completely agreed with him.

"Terrifying women are the best ones. I wouldn't tolerate a wimp for a daughter."

I rolled my eyes. "Okay, but she could be the exact opposite of us both. She might be into painting or something. Or maybe interpretative dance. She might turn into my mother and start selling essential oils at craft festivals."

"Heaven forbid." Lochlann touched my cheek. "She'll be a force to be reckoned with, that's for sure. But I think we're up for the challenge. Don't you agree?"

"Not sure I have much of a choice here."

His expression turned solemn. "You've always had a choice, and you always will. I don't want this to keep you from accomplishing your goals."

"I hope you know I feel the same way about you. I never wanted you to feel trapped."

"Unless you somehow managed to poke a hole in the

condom while it was on my cock, I'm not sure how you would've managed to trap me."

"Hey, I could've fished the thing out of the trash and gotten myself pregnant."

Getting up, Lochlann said, "On that lovely note, I need to go." He kissed me. "Be a good girl and get your report done."

"Yes, Professor."

CHAPTER SEVENTEEN

LOCHLANN

I'd never been one to work on my research with anyone else, unless I had to for some reason. I preferred to work alone, without the chatter of another person filling my ear. One time, when Sophie and I had first started dating, I'd brought her to the lab to see me work, but it had ended in a fight on the way home.

You ignored me the entire time! she'd accused.

I was working!

I should've known at that point that things between us weren't going to work out. Sophie needed more from me than I could give her. She wanted the kind of undivided attention that simply wasn't possible from someone like me.

Sophie had never understood why I'd found biofuels more interesting than her. I'd tried on more than one occasion to explain exactly what my research entailed, but she'd yawned and told me she had no idea what I was talking about.

How had we dated for so long? I thought to myself. *We were obviously incompatible.*

After Sophie had thrown her engagement ring in my face, she'd started dating an office slob that apparently worked barely twenty hours a week. Suffice to say they became the perfect match.

Today, though, I'd somehow agreed to work in the lab with Kate. I didn't have much in the way of a backbone when it came to her. Whenever she rubbed her pregnant belly and fluttered her eyelashes at me, I was a goner.

"It'll be fun," she said that morning on our way to the lab. "You'll see."

"I just don't want you to get mad if I'm not paying attention to you."

She gave me a strange look. "I'm going to be working, too. This isn't, like, a date."

I was skeptical. Maybe it was unfair to Kate, to compare her to my former fiancée, but I couldn't shake that feeling that the day would end in arguments.

When we arrived at the lab and started working, I kept looking at Kate out of the corner of my eye. She soon became immersed in her own work, only occasionally making some comment or muttering to herself.

I soon realized she'd completely forgotten *I* was there. Who would've thought I'd be happy when Kate ignored me?

I soon got lost in my own work as well. My mind had been so preoccupied lately with Kate, the baby, and hiding our secret that coming back to the rules of science was comforting. Science had rules; it had data, it had theories. Although things were always shifting and being discovered, it was always based on concrete evidence.

This thing with Kate? None of it was based on anything concrete. It was messy, entangled, and confusing. One second I wanted to throttle her. The next, I wanted to fuck her until my mind went blank.

Most of all, I didn't want to let her go. She'd grown crucially important to me—and that realization alone was terrifying.

I looked up to see Kate staring at me, a dreamy expression on her face. "What is it?"

She blushed. "Um, you just look so sexy when you're really into your work."

I laughed, albeit a bit awkwardly. "I've never heard anyone say that genetic engineering is sexy."

"That's not what's sexy, you dork: *you* are. When you're in the zone and you're confident and self-assured, it's super hot. If we weren't in the lab I'd totally jump your bones right now."

"Probably not a wise idea," I agreed, even as my body thought it was an amazing idea and that we should totally take our clothes off as quickly as possible.

"Yeah, we'd probably get chemical burns. What if you sat on the counter and burned your ass? That'd suck. And then how would you explain that when you went to the ER?"

I had no idea how her brain worked, but it never failed to amaze and amuse me. "Your mind is such an interesting thing."

She stuck out her tongue. "Interesting is just another word for 'Kate, you're crazy, please stop talking.'"

"That's not a single word. That's an entire sentence."

She threw up her hands. "God, you're pedantic. Why did I agree to do this again? Oh, yeah, I'm *helping* you."

"More like distracting me."

If she thought I was sexy, then she had no idea how sexy she looked, wearing a lab coat, gloves, and glasses. I'd seen plenty of women in the same ensemble, yet on Kate, it only emphasized how intelligent she was.

Kate rubbed her belly. Her lab coat was a little large for her, which effectively hid her bump in case someone came into the lab. Considering it was the weekend, there was little chance someone would join us.

"This baby is active today. Wow, yeah. Come here."

She grabbed my hand and pressed it to her belly. Her belly rippled under my palm, like a wave. I had to admit, I'd never tire of Kate grabbing my hand to get me to feel our daughter move. It always amazed me: just like her mother.

Kate beamed up at me. "Is it weird how much I enjoy her kicking me in the ribs?"

"Not if it's weird that I enjoy you almost pulling my shoulder out of its socket to get me to feel it."

She snorted, and I couldn't help myself: I kissed her. It was a brief kiss, not more than a second, but at the same time our lips pressed together the door to the lab opened.

We jumped apart like two scalded cats. Bloody fucking hell, had we been seen? Or had we jumped apart quickly enough?

"Oh, hello. I didn't expect anyone to be here on a Saturday," said Liz. She smiled at me and Kate, but the smile didn't reach her eyes. An icy fear curled around my guts.

"We wanted to get ahead of things before Thanksgiving," explained Kate. I couldn't help but be impressed at how calm she sounded.

"Well, don't let me get in your way. I'll only be here for a bit." Liz nodded at me. "Lochlann. Nice to see you."

Kate and I attempted to return to work, but the presence of Liz made that almost impossible. Kate and I both watched her, as if her body language would give us clues as to what she'd actually seen.

But Liz soon left with a casual goodbye, leaving Kate and I alone once again.

I swore in Irish the second the door closed behind my colleague.

"I'm going to assume that's basically 'fuck, fuck, fuck' in Irish," said Kate.

I didn't even laugh. I couldn't. I could only feel the fear that threatened to choke me. My career, my reputation—they could all go up in a puff of smoke because of one stupid mistake.

"I'm sorry," I said in a low voice. "That was my fault."

"What? No. Don't blame yourself. We were both not being careful." Kate's face was pale despite her earlier lighthearted words. "Do you think she really saw us?"

"I don't know. But we need to assume she did."

"So, what do we do? Just hope she doesn't say anything?"

I blew out a breath. "I can talk to her, see if she'll reveal if she saw anything. But I doubt she will. She's not stupid, and she hasn't liked me since I started working here."

Kate gave me a surprised look. "Why doesn't she like you?"

"That's a mystery. She did try to hit on me early in the quarter, but I'm not going to assume she's still upset about that."

"Hey, if I'd hit on you and you'd rejected me, I'd be devastated."

159

I tried to smile, but it was impossible. I was barely staving off panic. If Liz said something, I'd have to come clean. When Kate's pregnancy and our relationship was revealed, they'd fire me. Just the thought of being sent back to Ireland, leaving Kate alone to raise our child, made me almost collapse in sheer terror.

"Maybe we can get her not to say anything," said Kate.

"What, like bribe her?" My voice dripped with sarcasm. "Yeah, that'll end well for us."

"That's not what I meant. Maybe she's a romantic. It's not like we knew who the other was when we first met. There's that loophole. Maybe she's been in a similar situation and would be sympathetic."

"You think too highly of people."

"And you think everyone is an asshole, apparently."

Anger made my voice harsh. "You're too naive to understand how the world works. You're barely an adult, Kate. Do you really understand what'll happen to me if our relationship is revealed? What'll happen to *you*?"

Kate's face paled. "You don't have to be a dick. I'm not an idiot."

"No, but you're young. You think everything can be fixed with the wave of a magic wand. But this is real life. If Liz confesses to seeing us kissing, I'll not only lose my position, but my work visa will be revoked. I can't stay here to be with you and our daughter."

"What, you'll be deported?" Kate laughed uneasily. "That seems a little extreme."

"Not deported, but I'd need to get another job that would sponsor my visa. Which would be extremely difficult, considering the reason why I'd been fired. I'd have to leave the country eventually."

"Then we'll get married. Isn't that what people do when one person isn't a citizen?"

I groaned. "I'm not going to trap you in a marriage. And if it's discovered that we married for a green card..." I sighed heavily. "It's too risky."

"So you're just going to lie down and take it? Not try to explain our side of the story? I've taken you for a lot of things, Lochlann, but a coward was never one of them."

"I'm trying to do the best I can for you and our daughter. Believe me when I say that you don't want to marry me. Why would you when we don't love each other?"

Her eyes shimmered with unshed tears. "Maybe you don't," she choked out, "but I do."

Those words—they slammed into my heart. But Kate didn't know what she was talking about. This was just infatuation combined with great sex. Shaking my head, I said quietly, "I'm not going to hold you to that. Those feelings will fade soon enough."

"Wow, you really think highly of me, don't you? Too stupid to understand the world, too naive to understand what love is." She thrust a finger in my direction. "But you know what I think? I think if anyone doesn't understand these things, it's *you*. You're twisting the truth to suit your own version of the truth. And it's really not a good look."

"You can believe what you want, but that doesn't affect what's actually happening."

"Yes, well, since you're the big, strong man with the nice big brain, I'll leave you to find a solution. I'm going to go home and do silly lady things. Maybe I'll ponder how I manage to breathe and walk at the same time with such few brain cells between my ears."

After Kate left, I allowed myself a few minutes of self-pity before I began to think of some sort of solution to this seemingly unsolvable problem. Even if Kate hated me for it, I'd do it: for her and for our daughter.

CHAPTER EIGHTEEN

KATE

W hen I returned home to my apartment, I couldn't bear to stay there. Seeing Lochlann's particular brand of tea on my counter, his toothbrush in my bathroom, even the faded scent of him on one of my pillows, was painful.

Grabbing my things, I headed straight to my old place, hoping that Naoko wouldn't mind the sudden intrusion.

Isn't it kind of cowardly to sneak out without trying to speak with him one more time? my more logical side argued.

I wasn't in the mood to try to talk to him like a mature adult. If he thought I was some stupid child, then I'd prove him right. I was apparently much too dense to understand all the complex ideas rolling around in his brilliant, manly mind.

I grabbed the key I'd meant to return to Naoko, just in case she was out. I texted her right before I left, but as I drove over to her place, I hadn't yet gotten a response.

When I arrived at Naoko's, I knocked. Then knocked a second time. When no one answered, I unlocked the door and found my former roommate and her boyfriend going at it like rabbits on the living room rug.

A screech like I'd never heard before came out of Naoko. Henry was on top of her, his back to the door. In her shock, Naoko kneed Henry right in the balls. Suddenly the scene before me was like out of a horror movie: Henry, on his back, practically sobbing while Naoko was frantically searching for something to use to cover herself up with.

"What the heck!" Naoko finally grabbed a throw pillow and held it in front of her body like a shield. "What are you doing here? And have you ever heard of knocking?"

My usually placid roommate was breathing heavily, her entire body red, her hair a mess. Henry, for his part, had finally figured out that I was now in the apartment.

He grimaced but gave me a little wave. "Hey, Kate. What's up?"

Naoko got another throw pillow for Henry to cover up his poor junk.

As for me, I was trying so hard not to laugh that I'd had to turn around. If Naoko and Henry thought it was because I wanted to give them privacy, well, they were welcome to think so.

"Sorry, guys," I said. "I can go. I didn't mean to interrupt your fun."

Naoko sighed. "Just give us a second; you don't need to leave. Henry, are you sure you're okay? I kicked you pretty hard."

"I'm pretty sure you just gave me a free vasectomy, babe."

I heard shuffling, moaning, and Naoko's low voice as the two made it back to the bedroom. I sat on the couch, realized I was sitting next to the throw pillow that had been covering up Henry's dick, and promptly moved to the opposite chair.

Naoko eventually appeared, finally dressed, but not wearing her glasses. She blushed when she saw me. "I can't find my glasses. Can you help me? I'm so blind without them and Henry is currently recovering on the bed."

Naoko and I searched around the living room, even lifting up cushions of the couch and chairs. I began to peruse the bookshelf, only to find Naoko's panties in a potted plant. I held them up with a barely contained grin.

"Oh my God!" Naoko snatched them and stuffed them in her pocket. "Can this evening get any worse?"

"For you, yes. For me, definitely not."

We finally found her glasses under the couch. Naoko stuttered something that sounded like a vague explanation. As for me, I was just glad my friend was getting some from her boyfriend. In all honesty, I'd never been too sure about Henry's bedroom abilities. He'd always seemed too awkward to know where the clitoris was located.

In this instance, I was glad to be proven wrong.

"So, why are you here, exactly?" Naoko sat on the couch, cross-legged. "Did something happen?"

I sighed deeply. Suddenly, I felt ridiculous for running to Naoko's. I had nothing to be ashamed of; Lochlann was the one who'd been a giant douche canoe.

But Naoko wanted an explanation, and considering what had just happened, I owed her one. I told her about Lochlann and I sleeping together again, something that made *me* blush, along with what had happened in the lab.

"So you don't know if she saw you guys?" said Naoko by

the end of my monologue. "Maybe you guys were freaking out for no reason."

"I hope so, but Lochlann thinks she saw us and could do something to us. To him. He was really upset about it."

"Well, he had no reason to lash out at you."

"No, he didn't, but I can see his side, too. The stupid thing is that I'm just as freaked out as he is." I wrapped my arms around my knees—or at least tried to, given that I had a baby bump in the way now. "He might lose his job," I whispered, feeling anguished. "All because of me."

Naoko gave me a sympathetic look. "Do you love him? Because it sounds like you do."

My lip quivered, remembering how Lochlann had rejected my declaration, as if I couldn't possibly understand my own feelings toward him. My heart felt like it was being torn into pieces, like an evil little rat was nibbling on a piece of cheese. Except in this instance, Lochlann was the rat, I was the cheese, and I was kind of over being just a moldy dairy product.

"I do love him," I said, wishing I weren't so close to tears. Damn hormones. "And it's not just because he knocked me up, either. He's a good man. He's smart, and kind, and supportive, when he's not being a jerk-face butt-hole."

"I hope you called him that exact insult."

I smiled a little through the tears. Wiping my eyes, I said, "I should probably get back. I need to at least tell Lochlann that he's dumb and can suck eggs for what he said."

"Probably a good idea, although you never know: he might actually apologize."

Before I left, I made sure to check in on Henry. He gave

me a thumbs-up, even with a bag of frozen carrots cradling his crotch. "If I can't have kids, I'm blaming you," he joked.

I was walking to my car when I heard someone calling my name. A blonde woman strode up to me with purpose in her step.

It was Dr. Martin. Why was she wandering down this street at night? There was no way she lived in one of these tiny student apartments. Based on how she was dressed, she had the money to get a nice place off campus.

"Kate," she repeated, smiling down at me. "I'm so glad I ran into you. I wanted to speak with you."

I blinked in surprise. "You did? Why?" My heart was hammering so loudly that I was afraid she could hear it. I hoped, naively, that she wanted to talk to me about something banal. Maybe she wanted to ask for directions. Maybe she'd gone on a walk, had gotten turned around, and then her phone battery had died so she had to talk to me, specifically.

"Is there something I can assist you with?" I replied, sounding so formal that if I weren't practically peeing my pants I would've laughed at myself.

"Actually, I was about to go up to your apartment, but this works just as well." Her smile turned catlike. Under the streetlamps, she looked particularly feline: like she'd rip your throat out before you could blink.

Her words finally registered in my sloshy brain. "You came to my apartment? Why?" I wasn't about to let on that I'd moved over a month ago.

"I'd rather not have this conversation on campus."

"I feel like a lot of people use email for that reason."

She chuckled. "You're cute, but we both know that you

167

aren't stupid, either. I saw you and Lochlann." She clucked her tongue. "What a naughty girl you are, getting involved with a professor. Granted, he is pretty handsome, especially with that accent. I can't say that I blame you."

"I don't know what you're talking about. If that's all you wanted to say..." I moved to go around her and to my car, but her next words stopped me in my tracks.

"I wonder what the university will say when they find out a professor got a student pregnant? It wouldn't be good, now would it?"

I couldn't breathe. How did she find out? Had someone told her? Swallowing against the lump in my throat, I said, "What do you want? Because if you want money, I don't have any."

Dr. Martin snorted. "I don't need money, sweetheart. But you have access to the one thing no one else does: Lochlann's research. Give that to me, and I won't spill your secret."

"Are you seriously blackmailing me? Are you insane?"

"I'm just trying to make a deal with you. You want me to stay silent? Pay up. Give me what I want, and it'll be like nothing ever happened."

I lifted my chin. "You're assuming that I'd care if you told."

"I saw the way you looked at him. You're in love with him. The thought of him losing his job, his visa, everything? There's no way you'd let that happen. Not when you need him around to pay for this baby. They're so expensive."

She moved in closer, her voice lowering. "And when everyone finds out you messed around with your own advisor, what happens to *your* reputation? Do you think anyone will take you seriously? That you won't be ostracized from the program? Come on. We both know you're smarter than that."

I clenched my jaw so hard it ached. "I'm not doing shit for you, lady. You can go choke on your own bullshit for all I care."

As I got into my car, Dr. Martin said ominously, "You have a week to make a decision. I know you'll make the right choice."

CHAPTER NINETEEN

LOCHLANN

After the incident in the lab, Kate began to avoid me. I'd text her, but she'd respond hours later. At one point, she'd gone silent for so long that I'd banged on her door, terrified something was wrong. She'd looked at me like I was insane.

"Why aren't you answering your phone?" I demanded, wincing internally at how I sounded.

"Because I'm busy? I have work to do, too, you know." Her eyes were sad for a moment before she added, "If you don't actually need anything..."

Then she shut the door in my face.

It didn't help that I was torn between confronting Liz and hoping she hadn't seen anything. When days passed and nothing happened, I could almost believe it had been a false alarm. She would've gone to the dean already. If she waited too much longer, she'd have to wait until after the Thanksgiving holiday. Apparently Americans took their turkey and football very seriously.

Yet Kate avoiding me gave me a bad taste in my mouth.

As Thanksgiving approached, she only became icier to me. Frustrated, I entered her flat without knocking one Thursday evening. We had to fix this. We had a baby coming: we couldn't be in some emotional standstill.

You should probably apologize for being an arse, my mind said. *You never did, you know.*

I'd wanted to, I argued, but Kate hadn't let me near her for days now. It was like I'd contracted the plague.

Kate came out of her bedroom, scowling at my intrusion. "Did you even knock?"

"No." I looked her up and down, drinking in her appearance. She was wearing her usual t-shirt and sweats, her hair in a messy bun, her face devoid of any makeup. There was a red stain on her t-shirt, and she was wearing mismatched socks to boot.

Yet she was somehow the most beautiful woman I'd ever seen.

"You've been avoiding me," I accused.

Kate just crossed her arms and looked away.

"I want to know why," I continued, advancing towards her. "I've wanted to apologize about how I spoke to you in the lab two weeks ago, but you haven't given me a chance to explain."

Her eyes flashed fire. "Oh, when you basically told me I was a naive moron? Is that what you're talking about?"

"I never said you were a moron."

"You implied as much."

I let out a frustrated sigh. "Look, I should've handled it better. You *are* young—no, don't get all offended. I didn't know shite when I was your age, either. I'm not saying I'm some fount of wisdom, either, but I do have more experience in the world. You can't deny that."

Kate just clenched her jaw.

I gentled my tone. "But it doesn't matter what I meant: I hurt you. I'm sorry."

I could see the words slowly make their way from her ears to her brain, before her emotions got the message. Her clenched jaw unclenched, and she finally looked me in the face. But her posture still screamed, *don't touch me.*

"Apology accepted," she said in a clipped tone.

I sighed, pushing my fingers through my hair. "You realize what this means, right? This was basically a warning for us. We have to be more careful." My stomach dropped into my toes as I looked at Kate's white face. "We should end this."

"How can we end something that was never a real relationship?" she whispered.

I took her by her forearms. "We might not be in love but we have passion. We have sex. And we have a baby on the way. But if we want to protect her future and ours, we can't act like there aren't serious consequences if we get discovered. Liz seeing us was a huge wake-up call."

Kate extricated herself from my grasp. "You think I don't know that this entire thing is a hot mess? That I don't lie awake at night, agonizing over it? Some days I have to force myself to eat because the stress is so intense, and I *love* to eat. I'm fucking pregnant, for God's sake. I should be eating my way through the entire city of Seattle and closing in on the suburbs. Renton should've been destroyed by now from my appetite."

I hated that stress was causing her not to eat or sleep. I

blamed myself for it entirely. If I'd just made certain the fucking condom was a good one—no, if I hadn't given into my baser nature and slept with a girl I'd met at a pub.

I should've kept my cock in my trousers. That failure would now haunt me for the rest of my life.

"We should stay away from each other for a while," I said into the silence. "I don't want to, but it would be wise. If Liz is still suspicious, we can't add fuel to the fire."

Kate's chin started to wobble. "So I'm going to have to do everything by myself again? Great. Awesome."

"I never said that. I'm talking about our romantic relationship—"

"We don't have a 'romantic relationship!' We have fucking. You eat my pussy, you put your cock in it, that's it. Oh, and you get me pregnant. I think what we have is a breeding relationship, nothing more."

Red clouded my vision. "Now you're just being disgusting."

"Am I? Or am I being honest?"

Why was I fighting her on this? She was right, and I'd been the one to draw the line in the sand that this couldn't be more than sex and co-parenting.

But it hurt. It fucking hurt like a bitch. If I examined that hurt more, I'd probably see how much my feelings were entangled in all of this.

Kate had folded her arms across her chest, not looking at me. I waited for her to say more before breaking the silence. "Is that it? That's all you want to say?"

"Do I need to say anything else?"

I growled my frustration. "If you can't tell me what's wrong, I can't do anything about it. You realize that, yes?"

In an instant, the wall crumbled, and Kate looked stricken. My heart clenching, I took her hands, forcing her arms from across her chest.

"Kate, what is it? You're scaring me. This isn't just about our disagreement in the lab, is it? Is this about Liz? Because I'm fairly certain that she didn't see anything. If she had, she would've said something by now."

"She could still say something," murmured Kate.

"Yes, that's true. I'm not saying we're out of the clear completely. Just that I don't want to let what happened hang over us like an ax about to fall. That's no way to live."

"Isn't that what we were already doing? Keeping us, this baby, hidden? I've felt like I was one wrong move from destroying your life and mine." Kate's eyes filled with tears. "I don't know if I can bear it much longer, living in fear like this. It's terrible. I hate it."

Her voice broke, and I instantly took her into my arms. I murmured words into her hair, hating myself for putting her in this position. I wanted to do right by her so badly that I was tempted to confess the truth. I could deal with the fallout in regards to my career. At this point, that didn't matter: what I cared about was being here for Kate and our daughter.

"Hush, darling. Don't get yourself worked up. We'll figure this out," I said, even though I could hardly believe my own words. "There has to be some solution."

"We run away to the circus?"

I tried to smile, but couldn't. "I could resign," I said quietly.

Kate looked up at me in horror. "Don't you dare. You'll

lose everything you've worked for. I'm not going to be the reason you have to give up your dreams."

"It's the honorable thing to do. I should've done it the moment you told me you were pregnant, but I was too selfish."

Kate grasped my shirt, her eyes pleading. "Don't do anything yet. Please. There has to be another way."

I doubted that, but for the moment I let us both believe there was a solution other than the one I knew I had to accept. If I resigned, I could attempt to find another position. That would also mean I'd have to disclose why I'd resigned from UW. Who would hire me then?

I led Kate to the couch. "Wait here. I want to give you something. It's in my flat."

When I gave Kate the baby blanket, edged in delicate lace, I said, "It was mine as a baby. I finally persuaded my mam to send it to me, although she was suspicious of the reasons why."

Kate looked sad. "You haven't told your parents they're going to have a grandchild?"

"How could I without telling them everything?" I shook my head. "I will—eventually." I sighed deeply, hating myself for all the lying, the sneaking around.

"My great grandmother made this for her daughter, and it's passed on through the generations. It's said to bring good luck to the new baby." I pressed the blanket into Kate's hands. "I thought it would be fitting for our daughter to be brought home in it."

To my surprise, Kate threw her arms around my neck. "Thank you, Lochlann. For everything." She kissed me, and I let myself revel in the taste of her for a long moment.

How had this woman managed to take hold of my heart so quickly? It was if she'd cast a spell on me the moment we'd met in Ireland. She was a fairy princess, enchanting me completely.

"I want you to know that no matter what happens, I'm so glad that you're going to be the mother of my child," I said, cupping her cheek. "You'll be an amazing mam."

"And you'll be a great father. I know this baby hasn't made things easy. Things have been such a mess. But I'll never regret having that one-night stand with you."

I chuckled before pressing my forehead to hers. In that moment, I could almost believe that everything would work out all right.

CHAPTER TWENTY

KATE

I knew what I needed to do, but that didn't make it any easier. A week before Thanksgiving, I emailed Lochlann as my advisor to meet with me in his office. I needed a neutral place, one where we both remembered that he was a professor and I was his student.

Not lovers. Not soon-to-be parents. What we should've been all along: professionals working alongside each other.

If you're wondering if I gave Dr. Martin Lochlann's research, the answer is: fuck no. I wasn't about to let her win. I didn't fully understand what she was after, but it didn't matter. Her bitchery wasn't going to ruin Lochlann's life because of me.

When I arrived at Lochlann's office, it was a few minutes earlier than our appointment. Feeling restless, I began to walk down the hallway when I heard Lochlann's voice.

"Please don't forget to work on your projects over holiday," he was saying to his class. He was at the front, his shirtsleeves pushed up his arms, his hair a little wild. Clearly he'd been teaching a lively class.

I couldn't help but watch him work. From where I was standing, I could see both him and most of his students. Lochlann leaned against the desk and folded his arms over his chest.

Could anyone blame me for giving in and letting this man bang me into next week? He was so sexy. Even worse, he was kind, he was funny, he was smart. He even apologized when he fucked up. He was like some dream man I could never actually have.

The baby kicked me, as if she knew my thoughts. *I know you don't agree, but sometimes adults have to do things that suck.*

"Are you celebrating Thanksgiving, Professor?" asked a student in the front row.

In profile, I saw Lochlann smile. "Wasn't planning to, no."

"You can come to my family's Thanksgiving," a female student said before giggling.

I'd been so caught up with everything that I'd forgotten I would be going home for a few days. Our entire family generally congregated at our house, although luckily for us, that didn't include any random cousins or uncles and aunts. My parents' siblings lived on the East Coast, anyway.

The thought of Lochlann spending Thanksgiving by himself broke my heart, but how could he attend my family's Thanksgiving without giving away our secret? Liam would most likely invite him along, but I doubted Lochlann would accept.

The bell rang, and the students began to pack up. "Have a great holiday," said Lochlann as his students filed out.

It was then that he realized I'd been watching him. As his students filed past me, though, they hardly noticed I was there. It wasn't like grad students hanging around professors was an odd sight.

"Kate," said Lochlann, his voice curling around me like a warm blanket. "Let's go to my office."

My heart was hammering so hard when we went into his office that I was afraid I'd swoon at his feet. I sat down in the same chair where we'd had our first meeting, feeling like that had happened a million years ago instead of just two and a half months ago.

Lochlann closed the door behind him and sat behind his desk. Before he said anything, I said, "Thank you for meeting with me, Dr. Gallagher, especially right before holiday break."

His expression registered surprise at my formality, but he hid it quickly. Now understanding what I was doing, he nodded tightly. "Of course."

All the words I'd practiced saying, all the explanations, they disappeared from my mind in an instant. Suddenly I felt truly like some naive little girl who had no idea what she was doing anymore.

"I wanted to let you know that I've decided to transfer to another program," I said in a rush.

That mask Lochlann first wore when we met once again appeared. "May I ask why? This seems sudden."

"I know, and I apologize for just springing this on you. But I think under the circumstances, it's the best course of action." I swallowed against the lump in my throat. "I don't feel that I'm a good fit for the program. I've already inquired about transferring with a few other programs. There was one at Oregon State that seemed interested in me attending."

"So you've already made your decision? There's nothing I can do to change your mind?"

His voice was so cold, his demeanor so far away from the Lochlann who'd given me his own baby blanket, that I wanted to cry.

"No, there's nothing you can do," I said finally. "Me leaving will be the best for everyone. Then we can avoid any further issues."

I waited for him to say something, but he simply steepled his hands and considered me.

Then: "You're running away," he said harshly. "You've decided you'd rather run than face this head-on."

If only he knew about Dr. Martin's blackmail. He had no idea that I was doing this to protect *him*. I wasn't going to be his ruin. I refused.

"I'm doing what I think is right. If you don't agree, that's your problem," I said.

His eyes flashed. "It isn't right. It's idiotic. Why would you throw away everything you've worked so hard for? Tell me that, Kate. Because the only reason you'd do so is because you're afraid."

My lower lip trembled, but I refused to give in to tears. "I'm going to be moving out, too. I'm moving back in with my parents for a while as I sort things out."

At that declaration, Lochlann rose from his desk to stand over me. I gripped the armrests of the chair, feeling cornered.

"You're going to keep my child from me. Is that what you're saying?" His voice was silky but deadly.

So much for the pretense that we were professor and student.

"No, I'm not. I would never do something like that. I'm just putting distance between us because it's the best thing for us both. That's all."

"I don't believe you. What happened, Kate? What are you not telling me?" His expression turned to stone. "Is there another man?"

I reared back, stunned. Instantly pissed, I jumped up from my chair, pushing Lochlann back so I could leave.

"You know what? I don't need this from you. You're not my keeper. You're not even my boyfriend." I grabbed my bag and hefted it onto my shoulder. "You're just some guy who knocked me up. That's all."

It was as if I'd thrown gasoline onto a fire. Lochlann's mask dropped, revealing how hurt, how angry, he was. Before I realized what was happening, he'd tossed my bag away and yanked me into his arms.

"You know that's a lie. I can see it on your face," he said, his arms tight around my waist. He then tipped my head back so I had to look him in the eye. "You're lying about something. You can't hide from me."

"And I'm telling you that you're wrong."

Although his fingers were gentle on my face, the way he looked at me was anything but gentle. This was a side of Lochlann I'd never seen before. I didn't know whether I should be intrigued or scared.

Lochlann let go of me, only to sweep the papers, folders, and various office utensils off his desk.

"Get on the desk," he commanded. He began to loosen his tie.

When I didn't do as I was told, he said in that same silky tone, "I'm your superior, Kate. Get on the desk."

I sat on the desk, because I didn't know what Lochlann was capable of in this mood. *Or you think this domineering side is fucking sexy.*

Yeah, there was that, too.

His tie now loose, he went behind me and tied my wrists behind my back. I protested, mostly because this seemed a little extreme, but he just laughed at me.

"You think you can do whatever you want to me," he said, rounding on me. "You think you're the one in control. But I'm here to show you: you aren't in control. And you aren't going anywhere."

"I could always scream."

"Not when I know you're already soaking wet for me. I bet if I reached into your knickers my fingers would come out dripping."

I fidgeted, because he was right, damn him. My pussy was already pulsing for him, and he'd only tied my wrists behind my back.

Lochlann began to undress me from the waist down: my shoes, my socks, my jeans. He unzipped my hoodie and pushed my tank and bra up to reveal my breasts before he yanked my underwear down to my ankles. I let the panties fall to the floor and, in a move desperate to make him wild, I sat back and spread my legs.

"Fuck, Kate," he growled. He stood in between my legs, his fingers probing my pussy. "What a naughty girl you are, to show your professor your pussy like this."

I moaned when he just barely skimmed a finger through my folds. "Isn't this what you wanted?" I gasped.

"Having you at my mercy? Yes. I want to put you over my knee and spank you until you beg for me to stop, but..."

Suddenly he was having me stand up before pushing my chest down toward the desk.

"Spread your legs," he commanded. "Show me how much you want me to fuck you."

I had to bite the inside of my cheek to keep from moaning loudly enough that someone might hear. Lochlann brushed a hand down one ass cheek before he slapped the cheek with a cracking sound. I jumped, the bite of pain surprising me, before he spanked the other cheek.

"I'm going to make this arse cherry red. Because you think you're going to leave me." Another crack of his hand against my ass. "You see, Kate? I'm the one calling the shots here. Not you. Because you don't know what's best for you."

I was too horny to tell him he was being a pushy jerkface. Especially when he parted my ass cheeks, swept a finger from my asshole until it reached my dripping pussy.

"You liked that, didn't you?" said Lochlann in triumph. When I didn't answer, he spanked me again. "Answer me, Kate."

"Yes, yes." I felt like crying when he pushed a finger inside me, his thumb grazing my clit. "Oh my God..."

"I could keep you like this for eternity: bent over my desk, your pussy available to me whenever I wanted it. Would you like that? Your pussy servicing me, kept entirely for me?"

I'd never felt like this before: pain and pleasure formed together until I couldn't tell which was which. Lochlann began to circle my clit, and I felt myself growing wetter.

"Please, fuck me," I whispered, looking over my shoulder. "I need you."

His expression was animalistic now. Unzipping his pants,

he pulled out his cock and stroked it. "This what you want? This hard cock inside you?"

I whimpered. "Yes. Please." I wiggled my ass in invitation.

He flipped me so I was once again sitting on the desk. He lifted my legs onto his arms right before he thrust inside me. We both groaned out loud. I was already so close to coming that I had to bite my lip to keep from screaming.

Lochlann's gaze never left mine as he began to fuck me. His thrusts were relentless, his cock pounding into me. I wanted to kiss him, but I couldn't with my hands still tied. I could only capitulate to everything he wanted from me: my body, my heart, my very soul.

"You can't leave me, because you can't live without this," he said, his rhythm getting jerkier. Sweat had beaded on his forehead. "Your body doesn't lie to me, even if your lips do."

I wanted to cry. I wanted to come. I wanted to tell him how I'd fallen in love with him and that I was doing this to save him. But then my orgasm slammed into me and I couldn't talk at all.

Lochlann grabbed my head and kissed me hard as he came, too. I could feel him twitch inside me as he came in lengthy spurts.

"Tell me again that you're leaving me," he said into my ear. Now he sounded anguished. "Say it."

I didn't know where the courage came from within me. But all I said was, "I have to go."

The animal that had come out of Lochlann disappeared in an instant. He untied me and got dressed, handing me my clothes.

"You should go. There's nothing else to say here," he said.

Tears choked me. "I'm sorry."

"Not as sorry as I am," he whispered before he finally let me go.

CHAPTER TWENTY-ONE

KATE

Today was the day: would I re-watch *A Prince for Christmas* or *A Christmas Queen*? I'd already watched both five times already. Considering it was the week after Thanksgiving, there wasn't much to do besides watch Christmas movies and feel sorry for myself.

"Kate, are you seriously watching this again?" Mari stood in front of the TV to block my view of the opening scene of *A Christmas Queen*. To be specific, her belly was big enough to completely block out her and Liam's gigantic TV on the wall.

"You said I wasn't allowed to watch *Rick and Morty* at your place anymore," I complained, "so it's going to be all Christmas movies for the next month."

"Kate." Mari sounded serious now.

"You're going to make me miss the opening scene." It started with the soon-to-be queen, Kelly, accidentally tripping on a tree root and falling right into the unmarried king's path. Classic.

Mari grabbed the remote from me and turned off the

TV. I scowled up at her. Weren't older sisters supposed to be sympathetic when their younger sisters got their hearts broken? Oh, and their baby daddies didn't care enough to go after them and so they'd end up raising the kid alone, penniless and hungry?

"You can't keep just watching TV at my place and moping. You have to do *something,*" said Mari.

"I have been doing a lot of things. Namely, moving back home and trying to persuade Dad to let me use Dani's room for the nursery. Dani got mad when she heard about the idea, though, which is dumb because she hasn't lived at home in forever."

"I think she might've been upset that, out of everyone, she would no longer have her room," said Mari practically.

"It's the one closet to my bedroom, so it makes sense. So I need her to get over it so I can start decorating it. I've already started getting some things."

Ever since I'd made the decision to drop out of the program and end things with Lochlann, I'd thrown myself into preparing for the baby. I was almost frustrated that I still had four more months to go. If she had already been born, I could focus on her completely. I wouldn't have time to think about how leaving Lochlann had shattered my heart into a tiny million pieces.

Or how I dreamed of him every time I fell asleep.

Or how I was tempted to call him every day.

Or how I cried myself to sleep every night.

And now that I didn't have classes to attend, I pretty much had nothing to do all day. I had tried to help Dani out at the flower shop, but I ended up messing up so many bouquets that she had fired me after three days.

I came to Mari and Liam's place when I got tired of my mom hanging around me, asking me if I were okay. Worse was my dad grumbling under his breath about me dropping out of my graduate program for seemingly no reason. I hadn't told anyone the reason why. Not even Mari knew all the details. As far as my parents knew, I'd dropped out because I hadn't liked the program.

"I just hate seeing you like this," said Mari as she sat down next to me. "This isn't like you. You've always been the one busy with something. Even if it was something you shouldn't have been doing. It's just...weird to see you only watching these terrible Christmas movies."

"I thought you liked these movies!"

"I did, until you started watching them all. Why can't you watch them at Mom and Dad's, exactly?"

"You guys have a better TV."

Mari rubbed her belly. She was due in the next month. She currently looked like she could pop at any moment, although she'd only just passed the thirty-five-week mark.

"Are you ever going to tell me what really happened?" said Mari quietly.

I burrowed into the couch. "I don't want to talk about it."

"That just means you probably really should talk about it."

I blew out a breath. At this point, what did it matter if I kept it a secret? I was no longer Lochlann's student. Our relationship—whatever it had been—was over.

And even better? I'd told Dr. Martin that if she snitched I'd tell everyone that she'd blackmailed me. This meant that nobody had blabbed about anyone's secrets.

"Liam isn't here, right?" I said.

Mari rolled her eyes. "No, he's at a gig. He shouldn't be back for another few hours." She poked me in the side. "Spill before I make you talk."

I finally told Mari everything: my relationship with Lochlann; how Dr. Martin had seen us; her blackmailing me; my decision to leave the program to protect Lochlann.

"But you know what's the worst thing?" I said at the end.

"There's something worse?"

"I still love him. Even though he hasn't tried to contact me or anything. He said he'd be there for me and the baby, but I guess his word is bullshit." I wiped the tears from my eyes.

Mari let out a breath. "I don't know how you kept that all to yourself. That's a heavy burden." She took my hand and squeezed it. "But it sounds like you're at a point where the secrets are too much. Wouldn't it just be easier to come clean?"

"Yes, and no. Lochlann's position could still be in jeopardy. I guess I thought I'd hide away, have this baby, and, I don't know, enter the Witness Protection Program. I've always wanted to be named something more interesting than Katherine."

"I think you had to have witnessed a crime to be able to join that," said Mari with a small smile. "You might just need to live life like the rest of us."

I groaned. Right then, the baby kicked me straight in the ribs. "Oh man, she's been active today." I winced.

"She's probably mad at you for watching those stupid movies over and over again."

As the afternoon turned into evening, Mari and I talked: about babies, men, and everything in between.

Mari and I were in her bedroom, sorting through the baby clothes she'd gotten at her baby shower and listening to Ed Sheeran, when I said to her in a low voice, "What if Liz really does go through with her threat? And Lochlann loses his job? It would be the worst."

Mari got up to give me a hug. But we jumped apart when a low, growling voice said from the doorway, "Why would my cousin lose his job? And who is Liz?"

Mari and I turned toward Liam. Liam stared at us. I instinctively put my hand on my belly, which made Liam's gaze shoot straight to it like an arrow.

You know those moments when someone has that life-changing realization? Like you can see the actual lightbulb go off in their head?

That was what happened now. Liam stared at my belly, his eyes narrowed. Then his eyes widened as the puzzle pieces clicked inside his brain.

Well, more like exploded in his brain. My brother-in-law was hardly a subtle person, especially when he got angry.

"My bloody *cousin* is the father?" Liam's voice was scathing. *"That son of a bitch piece of shite! I'm going to fecking kill him!"* Liam was practically yelling by the end of his speech.

"Liam! Stop yelling. You're scaring me and Kate," said Mari.

I jumped up—as fast as one can when you're five-months pregnant—and grabbed Liam's arm, but he shook me off.

"I'm going to kill him. I'm going to wring his bloody neck." Liam rounded on me. "And you! Why didn't you say anything?" His eyes turned to slits. "He was your professor. He seduced a *student.*" He then swore in Irish for seemingly ten minutes before Mari and I could get him to listen.

"It wasn't like that!" I said.

"Is he already with another woman? This Liz person? Bloody, bloody hell."

I almost laughed, because Liam had no idea. Mari raised an eyebrow at me, as if to say, *it's your decision.*

"Maybe I should explain some things," I said.

Liam scowled. "Ya think?"

By the time I'd explained not only my relationship with Lochlann *and* Liz's blackmail, Liam's rage had returned. Now he wasn't listening to either Mari or me. It was like trying to get an angry grizzly to do a circus trick: mostly pointless, totally dangerous.

And since both Mari and I were pregnant, we couldn't physically stop Liam from going out the door to kill Lochlann himself for what he'd put me through. Not that if we'd been un-pregnant we would've had any success. He was a pissed-off Irishman on a rampage. Not even the Pope could've stopped him.

"I'm going to find him and he's going to tell me exactly what went on between you two," said Liam as he grabbed his coat and put his boots back on. "And then I'm going to rip out his guts and toss them into the Pacific Ocean!"

Both Mari and I winced at the sound of the front door slamming.

"Do you think I should warn Lochlann?" I said into the silence. I felt rather like I'd gone into battle and had just barely survived. I was almost tempted to check if I were bleeding somewhere.

Mari sighed. "I'm not sure it would make much of a difference."

I considered and finally pulled out my phone. Lochlann and I were over, but I didn't want my daughter's father murdered by his cousin. *Heads-up: Liam is heading to your place. He's pretty mad,* I texted.

Lochlann didn't respond. I even called him, but he didn't pick up.

Well, I tried. And Liam wouldn't really kill his cousin —right?

"I guess I need to tell the entire family who the father is," I said later after we'd returned to Mari's bedroom. "But Mom and Dad are going to freak out."

"Probably, but stay strong." Mari rubbed my arm. "You're hardly the first Wright sister to do something idiotic."

"Thank God for small favors. But I think this might be the straw that breaks the camel's back. Dad will have a stroke, and then he'll try to murder Lochlann, too." I scowled. "As if Lochlann seduced me and I didn't consent to the seduction. The pregnancy thing was just an accident."

"It doesn't look good, that's true, but if you explain, I think our family will understand. Nobody blames you, either."

"They shouldn't. We didn't do anything wrong. It was just a coincidence that he ended up my advisor."

Mari's lips turned up. "What a coincidence, though. That's like something straight out of one of those movies you're obsessed with."

I sighed. "I wish. If my life were like one of those movies, Lochlann would've already proposed to me in front of a roaring fire with a twenty-foot Christmas tree in the corner, kittens and puppies and small children gamboling in the background. It'd be so adorable we'd all puke." I sighed again longingly.

"You never know," said Mari. "You might get to puke over your nauseating engagement after all."

CHAPTER TWENTY-TWO

LOCHLANN

It started raining as I walked home. I'd forgotten to bring an umbrella, but I didn't mind getting wet. It felt good in a strange way, the cold and the damp. It made me feel slightly less numb. It reminded me that I hadn't died even though it felt a bit like I had.

Yes, I'd turned into a sad sack of depressing shite. I'd soon start writing poetry and crying to Celine Dion songs if I weren't careful. But it didn't help that there were reminders of Kate everywhere: a pair of socks she'd left in my flat; a note she'd written me that said UR A SEXY BEAST; and the flat she'd left over two weeks ago.

Sometimes I stood in front of her door, where she no longer lived, as if by force of will I could summon her back.

I'd since returned to teaching, throwing myself into my job. I went in early and stayed late. I took on things in the department that no one else wanted to do simply to avoid going home. Yet every time I went into my office, the memories of the last time I'd seen Kate were always present. In my haste to get inside her, I'd broken a ceramic pencil holder. I'd yet to throw it away even though it was unusable.

When I got home, Clurichaun seemed to sense how pathetic I was feeling and curled around my ankles. I reached down to pet him, but when I dripped cold rain-water on him, he yowled in protest and ran off.

Even my cat hated me.

I knew I had to force myself out of this woe-is-me pity party. I'd been wallowing for two weeks now. I knew that, and yet it seemed impossible to pull myself from the mire. I only seemed to sink deeper into it.

The ironic thing was that I'd been so insistent that I couldn't be in a real relationship with Kate, but when she'd ended things I'd lost my damn mind. I was sure some people would call that karma.

I needed to get in contact with her, at least to make sure she and the baby were doing well. I still wanted to be a father, even if I couldn't be anything but a regret for Kate.

I was making my nightly bowl of ramen—if I didn't die of a broken heart, maybe I'd die of a stroke from too much salt—when there was a loud knock on my door.

My mind instantly thought it was Kate. I threw open the door, probably looking like a fool, only to see my cousin. And then my cousin's fist in my face.

"What the fuck!" I almost fell on my arse, catching myself on a nearby table. I gaped up at Liam. "The bloody fuck was that for? Are you deranged?"

Liam just grabbed me by my shirt and shook me like a big cat with its prey. "You perverted piece of shite," he snarled. His face was red, his expression angrier than I'd ever seen him. "You think you can fuck around with my sister and get away with it?"

"Niamh? I don't even know where she lives!" Niamh was Liam's little sister; I hadn't seen her since his wedding in June.

"No, not Niamh, you dumb fuck. Kate." Liam pushed me away in disgust. "You screw around with a young girl and get her pregnant. And then you abandon her? I didn't take you for that, cousin, but apparently you're nothing but a heartless arsehole."

At that insult, I took hold of Liam and slammed him against the wall. He might have a few inches on me, but we were equal in physical strength.

"Whatever you think you know, you don't know half of it," I said hoarsely. "You have no idea what she means to me. What our baby means to me. So you can kindly get your head out of your arse and leave me the fuck alone."

"She means so much to you that you let her drop out of the program she worked so hard to get into? You're letting her raise that baby alone?" Liam's tone was dripping with disgust. "I never took you for a coward, but since you've shown your true colors, Kate and that baby are better off without you."

Red crossed my vision. I punched my cousin in the gut, getting a ridiculous amount of pleasure seeing him bend in half, wheezing in pain.

Both of us were breathing hard at this point. My jaw was on fire. Going to the kitchen, I grabbed a bag of frozen vegetables to put on the bruise that was forming. I had no idea how I'd teach with a giant purple monstrosity on my face.

Liam finally stood up, scowling at me. "I didn't think you had it in you to punch me like that," he acknowledged.

"Just because I'm a professor and a scientist doesn't mean I don't work out, ya fecker."

A smile crossed my cousin's face, but it flittered away just as quickly. He limped towards the couch and collapsed onto it.

"How about you explain to me your side of the story and I'll decide whether or not I still need to kill you," he said amiably.

"Before I begin," I said, wincing when I realized that speaking hurt my jaw, "I'd like to remind you of how you originally married *your* wife."

Liam scowled. "This isn't about me, and besides, I didn't get a girl pregnant and run off. So how about you give me a damn good reason why?"

I didn't need Liam to be my confessor, but at the same time, I hadn't spoken to anyone about this. Without Kate, I'd isolated myself completely. I'd ignored Liam's messages, including the one where he'd invited me to the Wright family Thanksgiving. As if I'd attend that, with Kate there. That would've been a fucking fiasco.

I eventually told Liam the entire story. He only interrupted me half a dozen times with threats of dismembering me very slowly. By the end of my recital, my jaw was aching like the devil, my frozen bag of vegetables was already thawing, and my head was pounding in my skull.

Liam was silent for a long time. Clurichaun, who I'm sure had hidden the second Liam had burst into my flat, had emerged from his hiding place to curl up next to Liam. Liam stroked the cat absently. I went back into the kitchen with another bag of frozen vegetables along with a bottle of whiskey and two glasses.

Liam let me fill a glass of whiskey for him, muttering thanks under his breath. He drank it in two gulps before he sighed.

"I can't say that I'm pleased with how this all happened," said Liam finally, his Irish accent coming out. "You should've left her alone. She's too young for you, and she had her entire life ahead of her."

I bristled. "You think I don't know that? That I hate how I've fucked up her life like this?"

Liam held up a hand. "But she's also not a child, and she lied to you more than once. That's on her." Liam shot me a strange look. "She also didn't tell you about the threats she got, did she?"

I stared at him in shock. "What threats?"

Liam rubbed his forehead. "I shouldn't get involved. I know that. I should keep my giant gob shut, but here I am." He poured himself another glass of whiskey. "Some woman named Liz apparently threatened Kate. I don't know any other details, though. You'll have to ask Kate."

I couldn't breathe. I couldn't even think. What had Liz threatened Kate with? Bodily harm?

No, Liz wouldn't physically hurt Kate. That would be too messy. But if she could get something that she could use to better her own career...that made sense.

My stomach turned. I could only think of strangling Liz with my bare hands when I saw her again. To threaten Kate like that...it was unforgivable. If she'd come for me, that would've been one thing. But Kate? She was innocent.

"I didn't know," I said hoarsely. I stared at my empty

glass. "Kate never said a thing about it. That must be why she dropped out of the program: to get away from all of this bullshite."

I swore in Irish. Liam just nodded in agreement.

Liam then gave me a serious look. "I'm thinking Kate wanted to protect you. Not sure how her dropping out would've done that, but that's for you two to discuss." He set his empty glass onto the coffee table, giving Clurichaun a scratch behind the ears, before getting up.

"I want to know one thing," said Liam suddenly. "Do you love her?"

When Sophie had asked me that question all those years ago, the words had frozen in my throat. Fear had congealed my insides. Finally, I'd said the words back, because she'd wanted to hear them.

And I had loved Sophie, in a way. I realized right then that *that* love had only been a partial love, but not for the reasons I'd thought. It wasn't because of my work, or because I wasn't capable of giving more. I knew the difference now, because the love I felt for Kate was with the entirety of my being. And that love didn't terrify me: it exhilarated me.

"I do," I said finally.

Liam's expression was wry. "Then why the fuck are you hiding out here? Go tell her. Now. She's been moping around our place for way too damn long. I can't watch another Christmas movie."

Kate, watching Christmas movies? She must really be upset.

But right then, fear finally slammed into me. I'd been so certain I couldn't have my research and love, and I'd told

Kate as much multiple times. What if I were wrong? What if I ended up hurting Kate just like I'd hurt Sophie?

"I told Kate that I couldn't love a woman and my research," I said quietly. "Because of what happened with my ex."

Liam looked incredulous. "That sounds like a bunch of bullshite, man."

"But if it's true and I break Kate's heart…it'd be terrible."

"It would be, because I'd break your legs. But just because you were convinced this was true doesn't mean it is. Besides, you can love more than one thing. More than one person. Love isn't a finite resource."

I had to stifle a laugh. "Since when did you get so profound?"

"Marriage," was his succinct reply.

Realizations were lighting up inside my mind like candles being lit one by one. By not giving up my position to protect Kate, I had chosen my work over her and our daughter. I'd been a selfish gobshite and the fact that Kate had put up with me was a damn miracle.

I stood up abruptly. "I need to go. Wait, no." I went to get my laptop. "I need to write an email."

Liam gave me a strange look. "Okay, that wouldn't have been my recommendation for telling Kate you love her, but whatever works."

"I'm writing my resignation letter, ya wanker."

"Well, in that case…" Liam went to get the bottle of whiskey sitting on my kitchen counter. "I'm thinking we're gonna need this."

After Liam left, I knew I had two more people I needed

to talk to. I glanced at the time, hoping that my parents were still awake. It was late in Ireland, but this couldn't wait until morning.

"Lochlann, what're you calling for this late?" said my mam. "We were just about to go to sleep but your da saw you were calling."

"Is Da listening?" I asked.

"Yeah, he's here. Do you want to talk to him?"

"No, I mean, yes. I want to talk to you both." I took a deep breath, then another. Finally, I said, "I have something important to tell you."

Bless my parents, but they let me talk once the first flurry of incredulous questions ended. I didn't give them all of the sordid details regarding my relationship with Kate, but I gave them enough for them to understand why I'd been reluctant to disclose to them the fact that they'd have a granddaughter soon. Even worse, having a granddaughter with an American woman—a woman who wasn't my wife and wasn't, to my knowledge, Catholic, either. I knew that that news would go over worse than my decision to turn in my resignation.

By the end of my story, everyone fell silent. I wondered for a moment if the call had been dropped, and I'd been talking to nobody the entire time.

Then, my mam said, sighing, "An American girl, Lochlann? Really?"

My da finally chimed in with, "It could be worse. She could be English." Then to me, he said, "Lochlann, you know you have our support, even if she's American. Or English. As long as you marry her. You're marrying her, yes?"

"If she'll have me."

My da snorted. "Don't be thick. She'll have you, if she isn't thick herself."

I smiled for the first time in seemingly forever. "I hope you're right."

CHAPTER TWENTY-THREE

KATE

Early in December, I received an email from the dean of the materials department, requesting that I meet with him as soon as possible. My stomach dropped into my toes when I read it. Although Dr. Calvin didn't allude to the reason why he wanted this meeting, it didn't take a genius to figure out.

I'd met Dr. Calvin on a few occasions. He'd been a quiet, almost stodgy man, who dressed exactly as you'd expect a professor to dress. Tweed jacket, elbow patches, oversized glasses, and a pocket protector for his fanciest pen. He'd seemed almost fatherly, and I hoped he acted that way in this meeting.

Then again, what could he do? Kick me out of the program? Too late for that.

I stood in front of his office door for what felt like hours, gathering my courage. Finally, I knocked, telling myself that all I could do was stay calm and answer his questions as best I could.

"Come in," called a voice. I pushed open the door to

find Dr. Calvin digging through his briefcase. "Oh good, you're here. Have a seat. I'll be with you in a second."

I watched him continue rifling through a stack of papers. Muttering under his breath, he pulled one that had been wadded up and attempted to smooth it out, but to no avail.

"Okay, sorry, couldn't find what I needed." He cleared his throat and sat down across from me. "I'm not going to waste your time, Ms. Wright, so I thought we'd get to the heart of the matter right away. Your advisor—former advisor, that is—recently came to me with quite a story. Dr. Gallagher conveyed to me that you and he had started an *affaire d'couer* in June of this year, but in some bizarre twist of fate, he ended up becoming your advisor here. Can you confirm this?"

I hesitated, not sure if this was some kind of trap. Besides, if I confirmed the story, would Lochlann lose his job?

Dr. Calvin sensed my hesitation. "Oh, sorry, I should've led with this." He handed me the crumpled paper he'd gotten from his briefcase. "Dr. Gallagher put in his resignation this week. This is his letter, if you'd like to read it."

Stunned, I took the letter. It took me a long moment to understand what I was even reading. But what stood out to me the most was, *Ms. Wright is an exceptional student and should be given her spot back in the program. She has done nothing wrong; I am the culpable party.*

"He resigned?" I couldn't breathe. "Why?"

Dr. Calvin cleared his throat. "Well, as you can see, he confessed to the entire thing. He stated that he was entirely at fault and that he shouldn't continue working here. I had to agree with him, even though I was greatly disappointed to lose an educator like him for something like this."

Why had Lochlann done this? Why had he given everything up? Not only that, but he'd made a case to give me my spot back in the program.

"I can understand if you'd prefer not to rejoin us here," said Dr. Calvin, "given what happened. But I want you to know that you're welcome to come back if you'd like. Dr. Gallagher provided me with the research you'd been working on. It's truly exceptional, Ms. Wright. You have a bright future ahead of you."

"Thank you." I forced myself to take a deep breath. "Um, can I think about it?"

"Of course, of course."

"Do you know what will happen to Loch—I mean, Dr. Gallagher? Will he have to return to Ireland?"

At that, Dr. Calvin's smile faded. "I don't know. As far as the university is concerned, we're no longer sponsoring his work visa. He'd have to find another employer who would sponsor him, which can be difficult, even for someone of his caliber. Add to that, the reason for his resignation..." He shook his head.

I had to find Lochlann. I had to get him to explain why he'd done this. I grabbed my bag, saying in a rush, "I need to go. Thank you." I rounded the desk and gave Dr. Calvin a tight hug that I knew was completely unprofessional. But I needed to hug *somebody* in that moment.

I rushed to Lochlann's apartment and practically ran to his door. Or at least as fast as a pregnant lady can run.

"Lochlann!" I yelled as I knocked on the door. "Open

up! And if you aren't home I'm going to be super pissed because I need to talk to you!"

I was knocking and yelling so loudly that the neighbor across from Lochlann stuck his head out his door to yell, "Can you keep it down, lady? There are people trying to watch *Game of Thrones* in here!"

"You should've watched it ages ago like everyone else!"

I was looking at the neighbor, my fist up to knock again, when my fist hit something decidedly not door-like. It felt like a chest.

Lochlann's chest. Thank God. And there was Lochlann, in the flesh, and I was so stupidly happy I could've kissed the angry neighbor.

"You're here. What took you so long?" I said.

Lochlann gave me a strange look. "I was taking a shower."

His hair was wet, a wet spot on his shirt. I wanted to rub myself against him like a cat. Speaking of cats...

"Clurichaun!" I pushed past Lochlann to pick up his cat. "I missed you!"

Clurichaun meowed in protest, forcing me to let him go.

"Kate, what are you doing here?" said Lochlann.

In the light of his living room, I noticed the dark purple bruise on his jaw. "What happened to your face?"

"Your brother-in-law happened to my face."

"Oh my God. I knew Liam had been pissed, but I didn't think he'd beat you up." I winced as I looked more closely at the bruise. "I'm sorry. Mari and I tried to stop him, but two pregnant women are pretty useless against an angry Irishman."

"I'm glad he punched me. He knocked some sense into me."

We both fell silent, the moment now awkward. It was like neither of us knew where to start. Thankfully, our daughter decided to kick me in the ribs. I grabbed Lochlann's hand and pressed it to my belly.

"This little girl says hello. She missed her dad."

Lochlann's smile practically lit up the apartment. Kneeling down, he kissed the spot where she'd kicked me. "I missed her, too. More than I can say." He looked up at me. "And I missed her mother like hell."

"I missed you, too."

Lochlann stood, cupping my face in his hands, brushing away the stray tears that had fallen.

"Why did you resign? And why didn't you come to Liam's to tell me?" I choked out.

"I resigned because it was what I should've done in the first place. I chose my research over you, and that was wrong. No job is worth losing you." He brushed the tears from my cheek. "I also realized that I was wrong."

I sniffled. "I mean, I hoped as much, but you're going to have to be more specific."

"I can have my work and have love. It's a choice, not a piece of my DNA, encoded into my genes."

"I could've told you that, you dummy."

He smiled, but the smile faded. "I can't guarantee I won't ever hurt you, or that I won't get so caught up in my research that you won't get frustrated. But I can promise I'll try my best, because you deserve my best. And so does our daughter."

"Okay. I'll try, too."

Lochlann took a deep breath. "Liam told me about Liz's threats, too. Kate, why didn't *you* tell me? I could've done something about it."

Damn Liam, opening his big mouth. "She wanted your research."

"I know."

"Wait, you do? How? Did Liam tell you that?"

Lochlann's smile was grim. "No, Liz did. I confronted her, and I told her I'd take her down with me if she so much as sniffed in your direction."

"I'm sorry I wasn't there to see it."

"She started crying, but I didn't care. That should say something." He scowled as he remembered. "That fucking witch. That backstabbing, evil *wagon*—"

"Wagon?"

"Hag, bitch, twat." Lochlann waved a hand. "The most evil of women."

"Oh, lovely. I'll keep that insult in my repertoire." I took Lochlann's hand in mine. "But don't you see why I didn't tell you? I wasn't going to be the reason you lost everything, and if you'd known, it would've all been over."

I shook my head. "You would've done something stupid and made the situation worse. No, it was better that I left the program entirely so I couldn't give Liz your research. But now you might not be able to stay here in America. What happens then?"

He took a deep breath. "Then I return to Ireland."

I realized then that I no longer needed to feel worthy by attending a prestigious graduate program. That I didn't need to show I wasn't just the prankster sister, but one who was smart and ambitious. I was still both of those things, of course. But I could pursue my dreams elsewhere.

And that uh-oh voice? It had fallen silent, because I knew I could trust my own intuition. And Lochlann wasn't an oops moment for me anymore. He'd become my entire world and the love I thought I'd never find.

"I'll go with you," I said suddenly. "If you have to leave, I'll go with you."

Lochlann's eyes flashed. "And give up everything and everyone you know? Leave your family behind? Your sisters?"

"I mean, it'll be hard, but it's just Ireland. Not Antarctica."

His lips twitched with a smile. "I love you. I should've said that when I opened the door. It took me too long to realize it, and for that, I'm sorry." He pressed his forehead to mine. "I want to make a life with you. I want to marry you and raise our daughter together. I don't care where that is, as long as you both are with me."

"I love you, too. So much. I'd follow you anywhere."

Finally, he kissed me. It was one of those kisses for the ages. It felt like we'd never kissed before, while at the same time, it was like coming home. He kissed me, telling me how much he loved me, how he'd resign a million times over to prove how much he loved me.

"You're exactly what I needed," he said, his hands delving under my shirt to caress my bare skin. "You're like some unstoppable force that pushed me to realize what I thought I couldn't have."

"Aw, are you saying I'm your gravity? That's sweet."

"More like *A chroí*." He tossed my shirt to the floor.

"I have no idea what that means, but I'm into it."

"It means 'my heart.'"

"Oh well, in that case, I approve." I sighed as he cupped one of my breasts. "I've missed this. You should show me exactly how much you missed me. Over and over. Until I can't walk."

He grinned. "Your wish is my command."

EPILOGUE

KATE

Once upon a time, there was a girl who had a one-night stand with her professor, got pregnant, and ended up moving to Ireland to be with him.

Lochlann moved back to Ireland after the New Year, and I followed him a month later. Moving to a brand-new country while pregnant wasn't on the top of my list of fun things to do, but I would've followed Lochlann to the ends of the earth. He was pretty much stuck with me for all eternity. He couldn't get rid of me even if he wanted to.

Lochlann was also able to get a professorship at the University of Dublin, where he'd worked previously. How about that for lucky?

I planned to apply for their materials program when I felt ready after our baby was born. I had enough on my plate with moving to Ireland and having a baby without adding grad school on top of it.

Our daughter, Fainne Lydia, was born at the end of March. (And for all of you who don't speak Irish—it's pronounced Fawn-ya. You're welcome.)

Fainne was due on March 23, but she decided to continue her residence inside me for another week. I tried everything to get my labor started: spicy foods, walking, and sex. So much sex that Lochlann finally had to cry uncle and beg for me to leave him alone.

(Just kidding. He loved it.)

So, labor story. On March 30, I was desperate. Lochlann was working a half-day at my insistence. I paced our little house while listening to 2000s pop hits (what's a little *NSYNC to get your uterus contracting?), walking back and forth, back and forth. Clurichaun sat and stared at me. I occasionally stopped to scratch him behind the ears.

"Bye, Bye, Bye" started playing, and I sang along as I began folding the laundry. With the baby a week overdue, we were pretty over prepared. We'd washed all her clothes. The nursery was furnished. We had enough diapers to last us five years, it felt like. My milk had started to come in, which was seriously the strangest sensation ever. I never thought I'd understand how cows felt, but here we were.

A sharp pain made me stop my folding. I took a deep breath. I'd been having plenty of Braxton Hicks, so I waited to see if I'd have another contraction. I began to time them, soon realizing they were spaced evenly apart.

Well, that must mean I was in labor.

"Fucking finally!" I said to Clurichaun. I grabbed my phone and called Lochlann. He picked up on the first ring. "I'm in labor."

I heard shuffling on the other end. "I'll be there in ten minutes."

He hung up before I could tell him goodbye, or God

speed, or "don't drive like a crazy person because first babies took forever."

Lochlann arrived in exactly ten minutes, his expression harried, his hair a windblown mess.

"How far apart are they now? Has your water broke?" he asked in a rush.

"Dude, it's been ten minutes. The only thing I've done is eat some gummy bears and pee for the millionth time today."

Lochlann drove about ten miles per hour—or whatever the equivalent was in kilometers—to the hospital. An old couple even passed us, honking in irritation.

"You know, I know I said first babies are slow, but we might need to get there before it's, like, the summertime," I said.

Lochlann scowled. "I'm not driving fast with you in labor."

I made him speed up when a contraction hit me hard and fast. I made him speed up even faster when my water broke, wetting my leggings and the seat. Lovely. I couldn't have broken my water in the hospital where some nurse could've cleaned it up?

Lochlann's eyes bugged out when he heard me yelp. "What is it? Kate!"

I was torn between groaning and laughing. "My fucking water broke! Ugh, I'm all wet. I just got baby pee all over the car."

He glanced at my lap, his eyes bugging out. He promptly stepped on the accelerator.

Despite my water breaking so spectacularly, Fainne

wasn't born for another twelve hours. She made us wait until the wee hours of March 31, the little bugger.

But when the nurse placed her on my chest, screaming like she was possessed, all red and squishy, I loved her so much my heart just about exploded.

"You did it, sweetheart. I'm so proud of you." Lochlann kissed me, brushing back the sweaty strands of hair stuck to my forehead. "She's finally here."

"God, she has your head." I groaned. "No wonder it took so long to push her out."

That night in the hospital, after eating my weight in pizza that I'd made Lochlann go get, Lochlann and I curled up in the hospital bed with Fainne on my chest. She'd nursed, peed, and had promptly fallen asleep. She was definitely my daughter.

Lochlann traced the delicate shell of her ear. "We made her. Can you believe it?"

"She's pretty much your clone. I don't know if she got any of my DNA." Along with her giant head, she had dark hair and was excessively long (or tall, depending on how you looked at it). There was definitely no reason for us to go on *Maury*, that was for sure.

"She has your personality," said Lochlann. "She peed on your chest right after she was born. She refused to come out when we wanted her to. I'd say she got more of you than me."

"Excuse me, you're just as stubborn as me. As far as the peeing thing, well, I'm sure there are some kinks of yours I've yet to discover."

Lochlann coughed, laughing, which made Fainne open and close her mouth. How was something like that so

214

adorable? Now I understood why people gushed over their kids. They really were amazing.

I kissed her soft, fuzzy head, feeling exhaustion take over the adrenaline of the day. "I don't want to fall asleep, but I'm also so tired I feel like death."

"You need to sleep. I'll watch over you both." Lochlann kissed my temple a moment before sleep claimed me.

Three months passed quickly, or as quickly as time can pass when you have a newborn. Fainne was generally a good baby: she ate, she cried when she needed to eat, she pooped, she slept. She grew like a weed. She thought the cat was the most fascinating creature in existence and had gotten close to pulling on Clurichaun's tail multiple times already.

I was getting dinner ready when Lochlann came home from work, Fainne on her play-mat in the living room where I could keep an eye on her. Clurichaun had already curled up near her. He'd taken to watching over her despite her grasping little fingers. I called him her guard cat.

"Smells good," said Lochlann. He wrapped an arm around my waist and kissed my temple. "You look gorgeous as always."

"I have baby puke on my shirt and I forgot to put on deodorant, but you're sweet." I patted his cheek. "I think you just want to make sure you get some booty tonight."

He squeezed my ass. "Always."

When he didn't leave to play with Fainne as he usually did as I made dinner, I turned to look at him. "Why do I feel like you need to tell me something?"

His expression turned serious. I was about to demand that he spill the beans when he went down on one knee, right in the middle of our kitchen. He then pulled a ring box from his pocket.

"Katherine Lydia Wright, today was the day we first met, one year ago. One year ago, you stormed into my life and never left it, and for that, I'm so thankful. Without you, we'd never have our amazing daughter." He opened the ring box to reveal a pink sapphire ring. "Kate, I love you. Will you finally make an honest man of me and marry me?"

"Oh, you're going to get so lucky tonight," I choked out.

"Is that a yes?"

"Of course it's a yes. It's a yes times a million."

Lochlann beamed, placed the ring on my finger, and then we joined our daughter to show her Mommy's new engagement ring.

And we, of course, lived happily ever after.

ABOUT THE AUTHOR

A coffee addict and cat lover, Iris Morland writes sexy and funny contemporary romances. If she's not reading or writing, she enjoys binging on Netflix shows and cooking something delicious.

STAY IN TOUCH!

irismorland.com
Iris Morland's Mermaids
Newsletter